VALERIE CARLISLE

Softly to the Quay

BY

D.F. & B. JONES

Grosvenor House
Publishing Limited

This book is published by
Grosvenor House Publishing Ltd
Link House
140 The Broadway, Tolworth, Surrey, KT6 7HT.
www.grosvenorhousepublishing.co.uk

This book is a work of fiction. Any resemblance to
people or events, past or present, is purely coincidental.

A CIP record for this book
is available from the British Library

ISBN 978-1-83975-333-6

FOR ANDREW AND IN MEMORY OF NICOLA.

Prologue

An agonising pain in my right shoulder was the first I knew of the attack. I heard, saw, felt, nothing until the pain.

Falling forward on to my knees as though in slow motion, I attempted to raise my arms to prevent falling any further. But my strength had gone. I fell on to my face, hearing rather than feeling my nose crack.

Now lying face down, blows seemed to come from every direction, and even to this day, I don't know why I didn't lose consciousness as my wallet was removed from my back pocket before I was unceremoniously rolled onto my back.

This was the first I saw of my two assailants. Two youths aged about 19 or so both grinning like maniacs and one, a fair-haired lad, snorting and giggling every so often like some braying ass. My other pockets were searched, cigarettes and lighter taken and my watch removed. They then left me, half on the pavement and half in the gutter while they jogged away, the fair-haired youth performing a childish skip every three or four paces.

I was now alone, the pain from every part of my body giving a new dimension to the term 'pain threshold' and I had difficulty breathing due to a combination of pain, blood and a broken nose.

This all happened around two o'clock in the morning at the bottom of a well-lit street near the junction of a main road. Unfortunately for me, it was also alongside a narrow alley where, I presume, my attackers were waiting for anyone walking or staggering home after a night on the town.

But I hadn't been staggering. I admit to having had a fair few pints after a committee meeting; nevertheless, I was by no means drunk or incapable. A close friend lived nearby, and I thought I'd try to reach his door, but on moving a sharp pain lanced through my chest. From that point on, my mind was a blank.

I came back to reality around six the following evening in the local hospital – my wife and a policeman at my bedside.

Chapter One

Today I saw him. The fair-haired youth. It was that period between Christmas and New Year, and I'd walked into town to collect an engineering manual, expecting the walkways to be quiet and the shops deserted. How wrong I was for the precinct was humming with activity and humanity. My wife, Jane, had warned me, told me it was always the same. There'd be children spending Christmas money, the world and his wife exchanging unwanted presents and most of the shops having their sales. But I, in my wisdom, thought she was exaggerating. How wrong I was I soon found out to my cost as I endeavoured to make my way through the busy thoroughfare.

The High Street and precinct may have been thronged with shoppers, but the pre-Christmas sparkle and glitter was lacking. Lights and decorations still festooned the area, but they looked tired, bedraggled and dejected, totally in keeping with the cold, miserable, drizzly weather.

Of course, there were the ubiquitous street traders and buskers plying their wares and musical talents (or lack of) from every available corner or section of pavement, which did help brighten an otherwise dreary day.

Then I noticed him. He was in the middle of a crowd, watching an exceptionally versatile busker simultaneously playing a banjo and mouth organ while co-ordinating with his feet and elbows the antics of two dancing puppets. I stopped so suddenly that someone cannoned into me. 'Sorry,' I muttered hardly aware of the 'Stupid bugger' flung at me as she passed on.

Anger and rage towards the youth surged to the surface, and I had great difficulty in preventing them boiling over. I wasn't surprised at the depth of my hatred, for I'd often wondered how I'd react if I ever came face to face with either of my assailants. What did surprise me was how hard it was not to attack him there and then.

He turned his head suddenly, giving me a sharp look, and I thought he'd sensed the venom directed at him. His glance didn't linger, however, but passed on across the crowd. I thought it odd at first that he hadn't recognised me, but on reflection perhaps it wasn't so surprising, for I was probably only one of many victims. Also, the attack happened over nine months ago, and during that time, I have changed. I'm not the person I was, either mentally or physically. For a start, my face has more lines, my nose is crooked, and my hair almost white.

Quite a large crowd had gathered by this time, enjoying the entertainment in spite of the drizzle and I merged with the spectators and numerous children; the latter edging their way to the front the better to see the puppets.

Moving to a position from where I could see the youth and observe without being observed, I wondered how on earth I'd sustained the injuries I had, for he didn't appear to lift his arms much less inflict such violence as I'd received. In fact, he had the appearance of what was referred to in my youth as a seven-stone weakling. The type who always got sand kicked in his face.

There he stood, a slip of a lad about five feet seven, with a pinched white face, huddled in an enormous sheepskin coat; seemingly unable to keep still for he was continuously moving from one foot to the other as his eyes darted constantly around the crowd. Whether he was looking for friend or foe, greeting or flight, I knew not. He looked so ineffectual that I began to have doubts about his identity.

Was it the youth of my nightmares? Why did I assume it was he and not any other fair-haired youth I might come across?

I had no answer only a gut feeling and the determination to discover, by fair means or foul, the identity of my attackers.

The youth moved on through the crowds. I decided to follow. A decision which turned out to be more difficult than I imagined; although in one respect the crowds helped, for I was just another anonymous Saturday afternoon shopper. Twice I lost him but found him again, both times coming from directions totally opposite from where I'd last seen him. The second time, he was pocketing some batteries taken from a counter in one of the three large stores we passed through.

That explained the capacious coat.

It was then I realised that although he appeared to be wandering aimlessly through the shops, he did in fact have a purpose to his movements, and that purpose was to nick anything small enough to go unseen into his hand, thence to his pockets – random choice.

Fagin would have been proud of him.

I was amazed no one else had seen him, but I concede he was very quick indeed. Here I was faced with a dilemma. Should I shop him to the nearest policeman or security guard! I decided not for by this time I was on a personal crusade wanting to discover everything I could about the youth and, if possible, his partner, before doing anything constructive such as handing him over to the authorities for petty theft.

We passed through the large covered market and heaven knows what else he picked up, but I actually saw him take a chop from a butcher's display as he ambled by. During this time, he spoke to no one and no one spoke to him, although he did wave occasionally, presumably to his other thieving friends working the same line as himself.

Reaching the open-air section of the market, I again had difficulty keeping him in sight and wondered why on earth so many people were out shopping. Perhaps they were stocking up for a New Year siege. Things became a little easier as the youth moved away from the throng in the market, making his way towards a line of bus stops on Borough Road.

There, any lingering qualms or doubts regarding his identity evaporated faster than hail on a summer's day because, with more space and less people, he was soon exhibiting that childish skip so well remembered from my nightmares. The skip appeared to be an involuntary action. No rhythm or method involved. Sometimes he'd walk several hundred yards before he skipped, but then he'd skip every other step for several feet before walking normally once again.

I didn't feel the youth knew he was being followed, although he still glanced round from time to time. Another involuntary action? Perhaps, or the result of a guilty conscience. Who knows?

Again, I found myself in the middle of a crowd, mostly women I noticed. Not shoppers this time, but bingo players. Passing the converted cinema, I gathered the afternoon session at the Mecca Bingo Hall had just ended, so I was able to mingle quite openly with the homeward players and shoppers.

This motley throng of shoppers, bingo players, children, one or two drunks, the youth near the front skipping round like the proverbial pied piper, and myself in the middle, all converged onto the main road and the bus stops. The youth walked to the front of one of the queues, oblivious to the mutterings and grumblings going on behind him, as if it was his right to be first on the bus, and no one appeared willing to challenge him. Certainly not me. Joining the back of the same queue, I was so intent on keeping him in sight that I only gradually became aware of the chatter going on around me.

'I only wanted number 50 for the hundred pounds.'

'He kept me waiting for ages for two numbers, and I still needed them when that woman at the end of the row shouted.'

'I never have any luck with Jason. Betty's much better for me. I don't know why I go, haven't won a thing for ages.'

'So, you won't be going tonight then?'

'Course I will, wouldn't miss my Saturday night bingo for anything and it's the National Link tonight as well.'

This interesting but enigmatic conversation was interrupted by the arrival of a bus, and in the general surge forward, I came to the conclusion that to be a regular bingo player, one not only had to have an agile mind but also be fleet of foot and able to work the elbows and umbrellas to advantage.

When I eventually managed to get on the bus, the driver looked at me with resignation and raised his eyebrows. 'This is the kamikaze run, mate, I don't know which is worse, the school runs in the mornings or when the bingo lets out in the afternoons. Half of them don't think it necessary to show their bus passes either. I can't wait till I'm a pensioner. Where to, mate?'

Looking at him in stupefaction it struck me that I didn't have a clue what number bus I was on or where on earth it was going. Not that it made any difference either way, for it was so long since I'd been on one that I was totally unfamiliar with numbers, fares or routes.

'All the way, please.' At least this way I didn't have to express my ignorance and was covered for the whole journey unless the youth got off after one or two stops, then it'd be an expensive bus ride. One pound, 50 pence later I was still none the wiser where we were heading, my attention being on the exit rather than on the passing scenery. However, the bus travelled quite a distance before the youth came down the stairs, a cigarette in his mouth and a sneer on his face, daring someone to object.

Waiting until the last possible moment before I too got off the bus, I reached the pavement in time to see him turn a corner about 35 yards away. Turning the same corner, I saw him jogging along with that oh-so-familiar skip which, together with other experiences, is etched forever in my memory.

I too hurried along the street becoming breathless as the exertion began to tell. Being of heavy build and so much older than the youth, the pace at which I was moving was taking its toll. He was almost a hundred yards ahead of me when he again turned off, this time into a side road and I stumbled to the corner in time to see him disappear into a house on the opposite side near the far end.

Resting for about 10 minutes to regain my breath, I smoked a cigarette. Not very wise, but I was more in need of a soothing smoke than I was of wisdom. Puffing away, I took stock of my surroundings and heaved a sigh of relief when I saw I was in Melchester Avenue. It was a name I recognised. I'd had visions of finding myself in totally unknown territory. But this area I knew well from my footballing days as a lad and young man, and although some things had changed, I knew there was a park at the top of the road, part of which ran parallel to the houses on the other side. The house into which the youth had gone would have a back door which opened onto the park.

With this in mind, and once again breathing normally, I made my way towards the park. Passing the house, I averted my gaze but noticed as I did so a For Sale sign affixed to the wall. Once in the park, however, I didn't have a clue what to do. It was far too wet to sit on any of the benches, I'd have stood out like a sore thumb and probably drawn some curious glances from the late afternoon dog walkers.

So, pulling up my collar, tugging my hat firmly over my ears, I set off for home, deciding to walk rather than jump another bus. I hoped during my walk to rationalise my decision to follow the lad and what, if anything, I was going to do next.

Chapter Two

I didn't do much analysing or straight thinking on that long, wet walk home. My mind was a turmoil of remembering. The agony of the attack, the pain, the mental torture, and how much the ripples had affected others besides myself.

Overriding all these emotions, however, was the word 'REVENGE' beating like a pulse against my brain. I tried to push the thought aside for I'm not a vengeful man, or rather I wasn't, but then I'm not the same man I was nine months ago.

My mind was no clearer by the time I arrived home, and this was compounded by a splitting headache. Whether this was due to the cold, the rain, the tension of the afternoon, or a combination of all three, I didn't know.

Feeling drained both mentally and physically, I'd barely closed the door behind me when I was simultaneously greeted by the dog, almost knocking me off my feet, and my wife who launched into a tearful tirade.

'Where on earth have you been, Tom. You look terrible. You've been gone for over four hours. Why didn't you ring me?'

One glance told me just how worried she was. It was written all over her face as well as showing in her hurried speech. Taking her in my arms, I felt the tension in her body as she clung to me. Not a good time to be telling her about my afternoon's jaunt.

'I'm sorry, love, I didn't realise how long it was going to take and I didn't have my phone with me.'

'What! Did you have to print the thing as well?' Her voice muffled as it was by the folds of my jacket sounded a little lighter. 'Or did you have to make the damn machine first.'

Thrown for a moment as she pulled back to look at me, I bent down to quieten the dog to cover my confusion. Then it struck me that I'd originally gone into town to buy a magazine.

'Not quite. But I have been looking at an engine. I met one of my old clients who mentioned that one of his machines was playing up, so I offered to take a look at it. I thought it'd only take an hour at the most, but you know how these things turn out. Always twice as long. I decided to walk home, hoping the air would clear my head of petrol fumes and engine noises, but it didn't. I'm OK, Just hunger and a headache. But I think I'll have a bath before I eat.'

I kissed the top of her hair as she moved away, wiping her eyes with the back of her hand. 'I realise I should've let you know, but you know me, someone only has to mention a dodgy machine and I'm oblivious to all else.' I lit a cigarette as much to stop trotting out more lame excuses as to calm my nerves, and to silently berate myself for causing such distress to Jane. Not to mention the lies. I caught her arm and pulled her close to me. 'Jane, I'm really sorry and I promise it'll never happen again. I can't bear to see you upset like this.'

Blowing her nose, she said, 'At least you aren't covered in grease and oil as you usually are. Oh, Tom, I was so frightened. Don't ever do that to me again.'

With that, she went off into the kitchen and I went through to the lounge and poured two stiff whiskies. A drink would do us both good, medicinal or otherwise. Taking Jane's drink into the kitchen, I was followed closely by Charley the dog, who appeared intent on making me feel as guilty as hell judging by the expression on his face. I'm convinced spaniels are the originators of the expression "hangdog look".

Looking more relaxed, Jane smiled at me as she sipped her drink, but I was feeling all the guilt, and more, the dog was throwing at me. Giving her a hug and a kiss, I collected my drink and took my weary limbs upstairs to a hot bath.

Soaking in the hot water and sipping my whisky, I once again attempted to put my thoughts into some sort of coherent order. And once again, I wasn't very successful. On top of my earlier turmoil, Jane's distress had upset me. I sighed and sipped my whisky savouring the warmth as it trickled down my throat. Like many others before me, I'd been the victim of a brutal attack and had recovered reasonably well from my physical injuries. I'd known the mental scars were still there but hadn't realised to what extent they'd affected me until my sighting of the youth in the shopping centre.

Why were my emotions so volatile? My body had been hurt and recovered so why not my mind? Was it male pride? The fact that someone could so abuse me, rob me, leave me bleeding in the gutter and go on their merry way without another thought. Or was it that they'd got off scot-free to do it again and again as they wished? They and other scum like them. My strength, my physical power hadn't stood an earthly. It'd been an unfair situation. Is any attack fair? My pride had certainly taken a beating as well as my body. 'Face it, Tom,' I said out loud. 'You find it so galling because you were unable to strike back.'

This had obviously been festering away at the back of my mind all these months. Thinking back to that night, I gave silent thanks to the elderly lady who'd been wakened by my shouts, although I don't recall making any sound, and had called the police and an ambulance.

I'd duly given my statement with fairly comprehensive descriptions of my assailants, plus a list of all that had been stolen, including my house keys. I vaguely remember the constable advising my wife to have the locks changed as soon as possible. Altogether I spent 10 days in hospital, mainly because of the blood in my urine, and during that time I spent many fruitless hours reflecting on what had happened. At 5'11, 49 years old, reasonably fit, broad-shouldered and quite strong, I'd often contemplated, usually on my late-night walk home from the club, how I'd deal with a mugger. Singular. I pictured a confrontation, producing my wallet and then dropping it as a ploy so that when he, it's always a he, bent down to retrieve it, I'd push down on his neck driving my knee into his face.

Life is full of nasty surprises.

On leaving hospital, such was my mental state, I virtually became a hermit, hardly leaving the house for three months and only then in an emergency. Consequently, my business suffered, and it was only through the loyalty and hard work of my foreman that it survived.

The police had nothing positive to report, although the constable who'd interviewed me in hospital kept in touch and still pops in from time to time. No one was apprehended and I became very bitter about the whole affair. My doctor advised me to see a psychiatrist because of my withdrawal from life, as it were. However well-intentioned the specialist may have been, I felt like a guinea pig, testing various drugs in the hope one of them would help me. None did, but the side effects were horrendous. My vision was blurred, I had singing in my ears, and either couldn't sleep or slept too much. Shaking, twitching, lack of concentration, poor communication and little or no appetite. Believe me, I went through the whole gamut.

Common sense eventually penetrated the fog when I finally realised, I wasn't the only one hurting, and I called a halt to the wretched hurdy-gurdy of an existence. I threw the pills away, dispensed with the psychiatrist and pulled myself together by my own determination. Gradually I re-joined the human race, and life slowly returned to normal.

Beneath the surface, the scars remained.

The ringing of the phone interrupted these painful recollections and I hoped it wasn't for me. I wasn't yet ready to leave my watery cocoon. But it wasn't to be.

'Tom, Tom.' I could tell by the excitement in Jane's voice that it was Sam our daughter ringing from New Zealand.

Grabbing a towel, I wrapped it around myself and hurried downstairs. A smiling Jane passed the phone to me and then stood in the circle of my wet arm as I spoke to our only child. 'Hello, Sam. How's things?'

'Hi, Dad. I've already told Mum, sorry it's a bit rushed but Tim's asked me to marry him. I've said yes and you are the first to know. We're hoping to have the wedding in about two months' time. Please, please say you'll come over.'

Jane was pinching my arm and nodding vigorously. 'Of course, we'll be there. Who else is going to walk you up the aisle? Congratulations to Tim.'

'Thanks, Dad. Here's Tim. It's a bit late, but he's rather old-fashioned and wants to ask your permission.'

As Samantha said it was rather academic, but Tim was obviously a young man who wanted to do things right. He came on the phone with a very polite, 'Good evening, sir.' I don't think anyone's ever called me sir in my life. He then just as politely asked if he could wed our daughter. I just as politely gave my permission, and after Sam promised to fax a letter through, we said our goodbyes, and I went upstairs to get dressed and Jane returned to the kitchen.

'Ready in five minutes,' she called.

'OK, nearly done.' Pulling my sweater over my head, it occurred to me that although she didn't know it, Sam's call had been very timely. It'd clearly lifted Jane's spirits and pre-vented me from spending the evening alternately mulling over my afternoon's excursion or feeling guilty about Jane.

As we tucked into our spaghetti bolognaise in front of the fire in the living room, Jane spoke in between mouthfuls.

'It's early in the morning over there. I wonder if Tim proposed with the rising of the sun.'

'For the moment you'll have to wait until you get her letter, and I'm taking no bets on the size of the next phone bill, that's if the thing doesn't melt from overuse.'

We'd known it'd only be a matter of time before Sam and Tim got married but hadn't quite expected it to be sprung on us this way. Our daughter was a teacher and had gone to New Zealand 18 months earlier on a three-year exchange contract. She'd met Tim, a New Zealand teacher, on the plane out and that, as they say, was that.

'That'll make the wedding sometime in February,' mumbled Jane, her mouth full of food, her earlier trauma thankfully forgotten, or submerged, under this news. 'When d'you think we'll be able to go? Sooner rather than later. I don't want to arrive at the last minute when everything's done and dusted. I want to be part of my daughter's wedding preparations. But I've that commission to finish and you'll need to sort out the workshop. Also, if we're going all that way, it'd be nice if we treated it as a holiday as well and do some travelling while we're there.'

'Slow down,' I said, laughing. 'Let's think this through fully and rationally if we can. There's no point going off half-cock. Hang on a tick, I'll make some coffee.' Collecting the trays, I went into the kitchen, aware that while my body was fed and warmed, my mind was working overtime. Vying for attention was the whys and wherefores of my afternoon's experience, my guilt about Jane, Sam's phone call, the simmering of an idea and a headache that was threatening to take over completely. Swallowing three painkillers, I made the coffee and returned to the living room.

Handing Jane her cup, I said, 'Why don't you go out first say in two or three weeks' time. You'll easily finish your work before then.' Jane is an illustrator for children's books. 'It'll be an incentive for you to get your head down now rather than leaving it until the last minute as you usually do. I'd follow a couple of weeks later. That way you'd have some time on your own with Sam for shopping and whatnot. What d'you think?'

Sipping her coffee, she was silent for a while, but I knew she was weighing up the pros and cons of my idea.

'I don't really like leaving you on your own,' she said at last.

I knew it wasn't that she didn't think me capable of looking after myself that was bugging her, but the old nightmare of the attack, especially after this afternoon. Taking hold of her hand, I said, 'Look, I know what's bothering you. Don't worry, I'll be alright. I'll have plenty to keep me occupied there's the business to sort out for a start. Not that leaving Jeff in charge'll be a problem, but even so there'll still be plenty to do. I'll need at least four weeks to arrange things. So, stop worrying. If we both went out so soon, I'd only be in the way. And don't forget, I'll have the dog for company.'

'Oh yes, Charley. Do we put him in kennels or d'you think Grace and John'd have him?'

'Grace and John, without a doubt. Well, John anyway, he loves having him around, and Charley certainly won't fret there.'

Jane and I talked a while longer, weighing up the ifs and buts without coming to any firm decisions. We watched television for a while and went up to bed about 11 after I'd taken the dog for his customary walk round the block and swallowing some more painkillers. Neither of us went to sleep immediately, each being absorbed by our own thoughts. Jane still hadn't agreed to my suggestion, but I hoped she was busy mulling it over as she lay quietly by my side.

For myself, I could only think of the opportunity this would give me to pursue my objective without worrying that Jane might find out. What was my objective? I didn't have a clue except I felt I wanted justice or maybe revenge. Those two words 'JUSTICE and REVENGE' brought to mind something written by Francis Bacon in which he said that revenge was a wild kind of justice.

Those few words about revenge and justice were beginning to take root in my mind and were to grow and fester in the weeks to come. They would evolve into something that would have been unthinkable a year ago. But as I've said, I'm not the same man I was then.

At that point I fell asleep.

Chapter Three

I surfaced next morning to the smell of fresh coffee and the swish of curtains.

'Wakey.' Jane's cheery voice penetrated the remaining fog of sleep. 'Come on, it's a lovely day. I've been up for ages.'

'Someone sounds bright and breezy,' I mumbled cautiously opening one eye while appreciating the fact that my headache had gone, and sunshine was indeed streaming through the window.

Easing myself up on to the pillow, Jane handed me my coffee before plonking herself on the bed. 'I've been thinking. You're probably right but I've still got my doubts.' Not quite awake enough to follow her drift, I made to speak, but she held up her hand. 'No, Tom, let me finish. I'll fly out ahead of you on one condition, which is that you get there at least two weeks before the wedding.'

Clarity at last. I nodded, sipping my coffee as she continued. 'After the wedding, maybe we could do some travelling, see something of the country and perhaps have a week or two with Sam and Tim before we come home. I'd also like to do a stopover on the way home, either Singapore or Hong Kong. So, with one thing and another, we could be away ten or 12 weeks. What d'you think?'

I looked at her for a moment over the top of my mug, noticing that although the tautness had gone from her face and her eyes were brighter, her hands were clasped tightly together. She was still obviously bothered by my prolonged magazine buying trip.

Putting the cup down, I took hold of her hands, feeling the tenseness, knowing for all her bright and breezy manner, she was still very uptight. I gently squeezed her hands. 'Look, love,' I said, 'I'm really sorry about yesterday and I'll try to never let it happen again.'

'There you go, hedging your bets as usual.'

'What d'you mean?' Looking at her questioningly, I unclasped her hands, slowly straightening her fingers until her hands were lying flat in mine.

'You'll do your best not to let it happen again!'

'Well if I say something is definite, it usually comes back to slap me in the face – but I will try.'

Jane leant over and kissed me. 'Yes, Tom, I know yesterday wasn't deliberate, but I was worried sick. You know what my imagination's like, especially after your accident.'

'Accident!' Putting a wealth of feeling into the word it came out sharper than I intended, but before I could say anything else, Jane put her hand on my mouth.

'Tom. Referring to it as an accident is the only way I can come to terms with what happened. Every time I think of what those bastards did to you, I feel sick and my stomach goes into knots. How people can do that to other people is beyond my comprehension. I know I'm not facing up to things but the pain's still too raw.'

By this time, tears were streaming down her face, her bright and breezy air washed away like petals in a storm. I was aghast and held her close as she started sobbing. Stroking her hair, I let her cry, recalling that, apart from the few tears last night, this was the first time since the "accident" I'd ever seen Jane cry. She may have shed tears in private, but for me she'd always been strong. Perhaps this tearful collapse of Jane's was an indication that I was getting back to my old self.

Letting her cry, I thought how crass I'd been not perceiving before now just how deeply she had been affected. There was also her language. Jane very rarely swore so when she did, it was all the more telling. Gradually her sobs subsided, and she was quiet with only an occasional muffled sniffle until eventually giving a huge sigh, she sat up. Picking up the edge of the sheet, I wiped her face.

'I didn't mean to break down like that.'

'Why didn't you tell me how you felt? It seems to me you've kept that bottled up far too long.'

'The main thing was to get you better, how I felt was secondary to that. It wasn't me who'd been beaten and robbed.' The tears threatened to well up again and she hastily wiped her eyes with the sheet. 'Ugh. That's wet.'

'Come here.' I held her close once more.

'Your chest's all wet,' she giggled, 'I must be getting hysterical.'

'That's more like my Jane.' I was quiet for a minute, then said, 'Speaking from my own experience, it's obvious that when I was going through my, what shall I call it, identity crisis if you like, the only one that mattered to me was me. There was no thought for anyone or anything else. My entire life consisted of why me? How could this happen to me? My feelings! My body! My belongings! There was no room to be concerned for anyone else. I wasn't conscious of the effect it was having on you or the burden you were carrying. The whole world revolved around me. It's only recently that I've been able to think rationally about the "accident".' I hugged her. 'And gradually I become aware that others were involved, especially you. But I was so wrapped up in self-pity I had no conception just how much you too were suffering.

'Words can't describe how I felt during those terrible months. It was like being in a black hole, no sides, no bottom, being sucked lower and lower. The only constancy was you, a glimmer of light in my darkness. Even so, there were times I was so low I was in danger of extinguishing even that spark. But you wouldn't be pushed away, you hung on, you pulled me through, and this is how I repay you.'

Neither of us spoke for a while. 'Hey, you're not crying again, are you? My chest feels very wet all of a sudden.'

Jane sat up; her face still lovely through the ravages of tears which were once again trickling down her cheeks. 'No, I'm not crying again, this is just the residue of what was left in the bucket. I feel drained but much better. I'd better go and wash my face. Are you going to wallow in that damp bed all day?'

I caught hold of her hand as she stood up. 'No, I'm not, as you so eloquently put it, going to wallow here all day. I'm going to change these sheets for a start and then cook you a slap-up breakfast. But before you go and hog the bathroom, there's two things I want to say. There'll never be a repeat of yesterday and, although I might not always say it, I love you very much.'

Tears threatened once more, and Jane hastily used the back of her hands to wipe them away. 'I know you do, Tom, and you know how much you mean to me.' Leaning over, she gave me a gentle kiss. 'Let's put the whole sorry business behind us, look forward to Sam's wedding. What do you think about being away for three months? We could even make it a second honeymoon.' Disappearing through the door she called, 'Mind you, it's so long since the first one I've forgotten what it's all about.'

'What are you going to do with yourself today?' Jane asked over breakfast as she munched on a piece of fried bread. 'I'm going to get stuck into the illustrations.'

'I think Charley and I'll go for a nice long walk and I'll do dinner tonight. But not wanting to spoil you too much, it'll only be sandwiches for lunch.'

'Sounds good to me.' She stood up gave me a long lingering kiss, a tight hug and was gone leaving me with a slight feeling of shame. Shame for the lies I'd told her yesterday and shame for the lies I'd undoubtedly tell her in the days to come. Most of all shame because I wasn't able to put the whole sorry unfinished business behind me.

It was around half past nine when we, the dog barking with excitement, drove off. I don't know whether my mind was made up before I left the house or whether it was a conscious decision but, whatever, it was 15 minutes later I pulled into the car park of Fromlington Park. Ours was only one of several cars for as Jane had said, it was a lovely morning, just right for walking: bright, crisp and cold. We started off walking round the perimeter, the dog darting hither and thither gradually getting his bearings in this, for him, unexplored territory. He roamed, I walked and smoked, mulling over the conversation I'd had with Jane earlier and as usual not making much sense from my thoughts, which were still inclined to dart here, there and everywhere like a phantom will-o'-the-wisp.

I don't know how many circuits we made of that park or how many cigarettes I smoked, but when we eventually stopped, we were at the rear of the Melchester Roadhouses. Staying in this area, I played 'fetch the stick' with the dog until we were both thoroughly fed up. Nothing had been achieved. No one entered or left any of the houses by the back door, and I couldn't remember how far down the road the youth's house was. What I hoped to gain by my surveillance was beyond me.

It also belatedly crossed my mind that I might be a tad conspicuous, a total stranger loitering in the one area for so long. So, we wandered down to the swings, noisy with cries from the children as they swung higher and higher, or dangled from bars and ropes, on past the derelict bandstand until we'd completed another circuit of the park.

On impulse as we passed the exit near to the houses, I decided to walk to the car park via Melchester Road itself. Putting the dog on the lead, we turned into the road and ambled slowly along the pavement. Slowly because we'd been in that park for over two hours and were both beginning to flag.

We'd not gone more than a few yards when two lads left the house with the For Sale sign on its wall and turned in our direction. One was the fair-haired youth, the other a dark, swarthy individual of around the same age. Drawing near, the fair youth glanced at me without recognition and carried on listening to what appeared to be a one-sided discourse from the dark lad. I didn't catch what he was saying for my heart was pounding so hard I fully expected it to burst through my chest.

I'd found both of them. But what next?'

Stopping to calm down, I realised I was outside the house. The road, which was quite long, was densely packed with turn of the century terraced houses and was, for the moment, deserted. But it was getting on for midday, people would be out and about before long, returning with the children from the park or going off to the pub for their Sunday pint. On impulse again, I turned into the small path and rang the bell.

After what seemed an eternity the door opened, and I was greeted by what can only be described as an apparition. A woman, perhaps in her mid-forties, wearing a frilly blue apron that matched her blue-rimmed glasses but not her bright red hair, purple trousers or yellow jumper, looked at me questioningly. Unfortunately, the overall effect reminded me of a demented salad. Whether it was the visual shock or nervous reaction, my heart began pounding once more and my mouth was suddenly very dry.

Before my courage deserted me, I did manage a croaky, 'Is an appointment necessary to view the house?'

The apparition smiled and spoke, 'Usually. Oh, what the heck, but the dog stays outside.'

With a silent prayer that Charley would be too tired to care and start whining and barking, I hooked his lead over a stub of railing and entered the house. Going via a long, narrow hall, the apparition gestured with a wave of her hand as we entered the "through lounge", originally two small rooms, now knocked into one. 'My husband knocked that wall through when we first moved here about 15 years ago. You should've seen the mess, but it was worth it. I'm Mrs Lythgoe but you can call me Brenda.' She walked away, still talking. 'This is the kitchen. I know it's small but it's very compact and bright, don't you think?'

Bright was hardly the word I'd have used, for each cabinet and unit was painted a different colour. Definitely not the sort of place to be with a hangover.

Hardly pausing for breath Mrs Lythgoe "call me Brenda" opened the kitchen door to show me the small yard with whitewashed walls and a bricked-off garden area around three sides. 'In summer, this is a mass of colour,' she enthused. I could well believe her. 'I don't let the boys play football out here, they might damage my plants, anyway they've only to open the back door and they're in the park. I'll show you upstairs now.'

Passing through the hall to go upstairs, I cocked an ear for Charley. Thankfully, all was quiet. Outside at least. I also prayed the youths wouldn't return while I was still in the house.

'This is my bedroom,' simpered Brenda.

Mentally shuddering, I entered the room. This time my eyes and senses weren't assailed by a variety of mismatched colours for the room was decorated in just one colour, which surprisingly enough was white. But she'd gone to town on the paintwork, which was purple and didn't really match the green curtains and bedspread. However, after the garishness of the kitchen, the room seemed almost restful.

'My husband, Ben, died three years ago, leaving me with the two boys to bring up. Of course, our Billy'd already left school, but our Shane was only 10 and he did miss his dad. Have you got children, Mr?'

Opening my mouth, I was saved the trouble of lying as "call me Brenda" carried on almost without pausing for breath. 'Boys are very hard to bring up. Not our Shane, mind you, he's a good lad, but our Billy's always done his own thing, gone his own way. He doesn't care for anyone except that mate of his Bobby, and now and then our Shane. Listen to me, I do go on, don't I? Along here's the bathroom and toilet.' (Quite subdued in lemon and green.) 'And this's the boys' room.'

After the psychedelic effect of the kitchen and the whistle-stop tour of the other rooms, I wasn't quite sure what to expect. Guns, knives, horror posters at the very least. But the room turned out to be the least spectacular in the house; perhaps because of the younger boy, and Brenda didn't enlighten me. It was rather small with two bunk beds, the usual football posters, Liverpool and Manchester United, pictures of partly clad females and some pennants.

I was disappointed. But what was I expecting? Evidence plastered or littered all around the room? Evidence of what? Drugs, empty aerosol cans, ill-gotten souvenirs such as my wallet?

Obviously, I wasn't thinking straight. Billy Lythgoe would have to be a complete moron to litter his home with the detritus of his and Bobby's life, especially with his younger brother around. But whether it was through concern for Shane or self-preservation, total moron he apparently was not.

Mrs Lythgoe's voiced penetrated my thoughts, and we returned downstairs to the through lounge. 'Now the price has been reduced from 69,000 down to 65 and a half for a quick sale. My mother's left me her three-bedroomed semi in Berrington Avenue. D'you know it at all? It's by the new Civic Centre in Monkton, a much better area for our Shane to grow up in. Mind you, our Billy doesn't want to go, but he's a law unto himself anyway. Not that there's anything wrong with this area and this house is ideal for a first-time buyer or anyone who wants a small place. But the other house has so much more potential.'

I cringed at the thought of "call me Brenda" at large in a three-bedroomed semi with "potential" and a lethal paintbrush in her hand. Other thoughts began to invade my mind such as how long I'd been in the house, which seemed an eternity but, in fact, after a surreptitious glance at my watch, proved to have been only 15 minutes. I was also fully expecting the youths to return at any moment. As these thoughts were racing through my mind, I'd been absently staring at some photographs without really seeing them until Brenda said, 'That's me and Ben on our wedding day.'

I was surprised to see that she'd been a normal bride, all in white and really quite pretty. Perhaps she was a late developer in the psychedelic department. Then I saw them, amongst a group of school and holiday photos. A coloured snap of the two of them. The fair-haired youth had his arm across the shoulders of the dark, swarthy looking lad. The two I'd passed in the road.

'They look good friends,' I said, picking up the photo to satisfy myself once again that the dark youth had indeed been my other assailant.

'Yea that's our Billy with his mate Bobby. Just gone out they have, nearly always together they are. I don't know whether his mother's had to put up with the things from him that I've had to from our Billy. Broke my heart that lad has many a time. Never wanted for nothing has our Billy, but never satisfied. Always wanting more and what he's not given he takes. Sometimes I wonder if he's really mine. You hear about babies being mixed up in hospitals, don't you? Still, we all have our crosses to bear and he's mine, but our Shane compensates for all of our Billy's faults.'

Very anxious to take my leave, I edged my way down the hall. 'I'll have to go now; I promised my wife I'd be back before 12. It's late I know, but the opportunity to see over your house was too good to miss and I'm sure my wife'll be very interested. Especially as it's such a bargain. Thank you very much, you've been so kind.'

I was babbling and knew it. It was a miracle I managed to say even that much for "call me Brenda" was still waffling on about wayward children as I bent down to slip Charley's leash from the railing stub. He'd been asleep, and grumbling as usual, got slowly to his feet with a mournful look on his face.

Shaking Mrs Lythgoe's hand and thanking her profusely once again, I walked off down the street as fast as decency and the complaining dog would allow. I breathed a sigh of relief as much for the absence of verbal and visual assault to my senses, as for the fact that the youths hadn't returned while I was there.

Maybe I'd only have been someone looking over the house, but it was important that they shouldn't become aware of me whatsoever. The feeling was there that if I hung around the area much longer, Billy at least could become suspicious and perhaps make connections. After all, it was only 24 hours ago that I'd followed him all the way through town, onto a bus, almost to his front door.

Smiling to myself, I wondered if Brenda would ever be quiet long enough for anyone to make her an offer for the house. I'd managed to take my leave of her without even giving my name, much less the area where I lived. At least in this instance, her volubility had saved me from the necessity of further lies.

Retrieving my car, I noticed there were still plenty of vehicles around, for which I was thankful. The park appeared to be a popular place for Sunday morning activities, so I hoped that neither myself nor the car or even the dog would have attracted much attention. Why was I so concerned with anonymity all of a sudden? What were my motives in going to the park in the first place, and the crazier action of going around the house?

There was no ready answer and driving home, Charley's snores from the back seat prevented any sensible thoughts I might've had. Those snores, coupled with the after-effects to my eyes and ears from "call me Brenda", were enough for any man to cope with in one day.

Chapter Four

Standing in the kitchen preparing sandwiches for lunch, I knew I needed to think and reflect. Firstly, why I'd gone to the park, and more bizarrely, what possessed me to go round that house. I pulled myself up short. That's all I appeared to be doing, telling myself I must think, must reason, must explain.

So far, no rational thinking had been achieved in any shape or form. I'd simply been lurching from one irrational step to another. That must stop. I tried to convince myself that if I was to discover anything about the two young thugs, then I had to be dispassionate and not let anger and hatred intrude to the extent that I was blinded to any constructive actions and thoughts.

Reaching for a slice of meat, I was surprised to find there was none left and looking at the pile of sandwiches on my left, I laughed out loud. I'd been so carried away by my musings, I'd merrily made sandwich after sandwich after sandwich. Looking ruefully at the pile, I wondered if it could be classed as constructive action – a construction certainly, no doubt about that.

While my mind had been busy building nothing from my cotton wool thoughts, my hands had been even busier. There before me was a plate of sandwiches of tower proportions, threatening any minute to topple over on to the kitchen floor. Putting several on to a smaller plate, I placed the rest in the fridge. They'd get eaten sooner or later, by the dog if not by us.

'Jane,' I called, 'it's ready. Do you want tea or coffee?'

'Tea please,' she replied coming down from her studio, an abstract expression on her face, which meant she was still

24

mentally working on her illustrations. Her dark hair was tied back, and she had a pencil behind each ear. Munching her way through her third sandwich, she said, 'If I work every day this week, and there's no reason why I shouldn't, I could be finished by next Monday.' Picking up another sandwich, she continued, 'That's if I can overcome the tricky bit I'm working on at the moment. The heads just won't sit right. Oh well, sometimes a break's all that's needed, and I certainly needed a cuppa. So, where'd you go? Long walk judging by the dog.'

The dog was slumped on the floor fighting sleep in case he missed any titbits. The phone rang. Saved by the bell. The old cliché came to mind as I went to answer it. It was Jane's friend Margaret and I smiled as I handed over the phone. That call would take up most if not all of Jane's allotted break. Hopefully by then she'd have forgotten about my walk and save me the embarrassment of lying again.

When I was a small boy, my grandmother often said that liars were anathema to her. (Not that I understood what anathema meant way back then, but I certainly understood the gist of it.) She'd rather have had a thief than a liar. Her argument being that you knew where you were with a thief. I wonder what she'd have made of my two thieves and my new-found propensity for lying.

How could I tell my wife that I'd spent the morning walking round and round an unfamiliar park and viewed a totally unsuitable house in a totally unsuitable neighbourhood when we had no intention whatsoever of moving. Jane would rapidly come to the conclusion, perhaps rightly so, that I was either regressing once more into a confused mental state but with different symptoms, or I'd finally flipped my lid altogether. That'd definitely put the kybosh on her solo trip. She'd stick to my side like superglue and make sure we boarded that plane together.

Surprisingly, it was quite a short phone call.

'She's in the middle of cooking dinner,' said Jane by way of explanation.

'She must be catering for some very important visitors,' I replied. 'I've never known a simple matter of cooking a meal interrupt one of Margaret's telephone calls.'

Jane laughed but didn't rise to the bait of defending her friend. Instead, she poured herself a fresh cup of tea and bit into another sandwich before reverting to her earlier thoughts. Fortunately, these didn't include my morning jaunts but centred once more around her work and our trip.

'Hopefully, I'll finish this work with a couple of weeks to spare, which'll give us time to get tickets, visas, presents and the thousand and one things that'll need doing. Not to mention new clothes.' She eyed my shapeless old sweater, which she'd threatened with extinction many times. 'For both of us. It's summer over there remember.' Her mind jumped another notch. 'We will be able to get seats at such short notice, won't we?'

'Of course, we will. Even if you have to go via Outer Mongolia, you'll be on a plane in three weeks' time.'

'Are you in a hurry to get rid of me, Tom Marshall?'

'Of course.' I grinned. 'Just think of it. No cold feet in bed, no complaints about my sartorial appearance.' I poked a finger through a hole in my jumper to emphasise my point. 'Charley sleeping on the furniture, unwashed dishes, wild parties, the list is endless. But, joking aside, I wouldn't rely too much on being free by that Monday if I were you.'

'Why not? You know I can work straight through if I've got to.'

'It's not that, but it's New Year's Eve tomorrow night, and if previous years are any yardstick, neither of us'll feel like moving a muscle, much less one of us getting down to delicate artwork. And if I remember correctly, last year a certain one of us was incapacitated for two whole days.'

'So I was, though I still swear someone spiked my drinks and you can take that sceptical look off your face. It was a great night, wasn't it? All the hopes and dreams we had. We thought we were going to have a marvellous year.' She sighed. 'And look what happened.'

Giving a shudder she said no more on the subject, instead asked if there was any more tea in the pot.

'I'll make a fresh brew.' Giving her shoulder a reassuring squeeze, I went into the kitchen. Waiting for the kettle to boil, I called, 'As I'm not going back to work until the ninth, I'll volunteer to be mine host, bottle washer and dog carer, so you can concentrate on your work. I'll just need to pop into the workshop on Wednesday to do a few bits and see if Sam's faxed that letter through.'

Jane came into the kitchen, pushing the hair that had escaped its confinement away from her forehead. A trait Sam also had, for although our daughter is supposed to resemble me, she has a lot of her mother's mannerisms and expressions.

'I wonder if Sam'll settle over there,' she said. 'It's a bit far for a weekend visit, isn't it? Perhaps Tim'd like to live over here, but that'd leave his parents in the same situation. Still, the world's a much smaller place than it used to be, perhaps more accessible would be a better way of putting it.' She picked up her mug of tea. 'Right, I'm off back to the drawing board – no pun intended. I'll take this with me.' Brushing her fingers across my arm, she blew me a kiss and vanished through the door, humming quietly as she made her way upstairs to her studio.

Collecting the dishes from the dining room and dumping them in the sink, I proceeded to wash up. The dog, curled up in his basket, opened one eye, looked at me and closed it again. 'I know exactly how you feel, old boy, we're not used to so much exercise in one go are we, and neither of us is in the first flush of youth either. Or the second flush for that matter.'

Making a cup of coffee, I took it through to the lounge, settled into my chair and put my feet up. Normally Charley would've followed me into the room, curling up alongside my chair, but he'd not even bothered to move from his basket. He was definitely very, very tired, I thought, sitting back, cradling my cup in both hands.

Feeling rather weary myself, I nevertheless cast my mind to
the supposedly constructive thinking I'd been on about earlier
in the kitchen. I'd explained to myself my motive for following
the fair-haired youth the previous day. But why on earth did I
spend this morning wandering round a park several miles
away from home when there was a perfectly adequate park no
more than five minutes' walk away. And, what possessed me
to enter that house! We're not in the market for a house, and if
we were, it wouldn't be for the totally unsuitable residence I'd
visited that morning.

Sipping my coffee reflectively, another thought popped into
my head. I'd not wanted to be noticed by anyone in the area.
Why? If that was the case, I hadn't gone about it very
unobtrusively. After the morning's performance, it's a wonder
my description and actions weren't imprinted on everyone
who was in that park, especially when accompanied by a dog.
Dog owners tend to remember other dog owners, or perhaps
they remember the dogs first and the owners next.

Casting my mind back to the park, I found that by recalling
the dogs I was able to picture almost all of the owners. If I was
able to do that, then I'm sure others would recall a very
friendly, active (for the first couple of hours at least), black
and white springer spaniel called Charley, who with his owner
was a stranger to Fromlington Park. It wouldn't be a good
idea to repeat that exercise too often. I don't think "Call me
Brenda" would forget us either.

I gave myself a mental shake. Something was brewing deep
in the dark recesses of my mind. I mightn't quite know what it
was, but the certainty that I wanted to remain an unknown
factor was perhaps an indication that I wanted to go back to
that area. Also, perhaps the reason there wasn't much
constructive thinking going on could be because I was
frightened to admit to myself what exactly was stirring in the
depths of my subconscious.

The bile rose in my throat as I thought of those two.
Initially, I knew I wanted to find out where Bobby lived and

then discover everything possible about both of them. Their habits, drugs or otherwise. Friends – if they had any. Then maybe I'd decide whether to go to the police or take some other course of action. However, in order to do any ferreting, it would be necessary to be as unobtrusive as possible.

I reminded myself of a 1930s detective novelist, making a list of clues in order to discern the wood from the trees. I smiled grimly. In my case they weren't clues, but steps that had to be taken before any form of progress could be made.

The first step was to be able to come, go and manoeuvre without giving Jane cause for suspicion or alarm, thereby avoiding unnecessary worry on her behalf. So, I couldn't do anything until she went off to New Zealand. There was also the little matter of sorting out my own business affairs if I was going to be out of the country for three months. The business was only just getting back on a level footing after my prolonged absence and I didn't intend to let it slide again, as it had because of those two rats.

Jeff Fletcher is my competent right-hand man. He'd worked wonders to stop the firm folding altogether when I was at my worst and past caring. I owed him. One of the debts I could repay would be by doing as much of the paperwork as possible before going and giving him all the authority he needed to run the business. In other words, to leave the reins fully in his hands once again but this time with the clout to drive the wagon. My small engineering business had been built up over the last 25 years and gave me a reasonable living as well as providing work for my six employees. Four of whom had been with me for at least 15 years. The plant was closed for the Christmas and New Year break until the ninth of January, so I'd not be able to achieve much before then. Neither could I ring Jeff for he was at his son's in Scotland until Thursday, but I knew he'd be delighted by the news of Sam's wedding. He had a very soft spot for her.

'What happened to mine host. Asleep on the job?'

Those words ringing in my ears woke me with a start. I hadn't realised I was nodding off much less that I'd been asleep for almost two hours. At least I'd had the forethought to place the half-filled mug of coffee on the floor.

Jane was standing in the doorway, although she'd not as yet put on the lights or drawn the curtains.

'Kettle's on. I'm done for the day. Thankfully, the heads are now coming along nicely. I'm just going to freshen up. Perhaps we can have a drink and then decide whether to eat in, get a takeaway or eat out.' She snorted. 'Though judging by both you and the dog, I think it'll be a takeaway. That was some walk you had today. Where on earth did you go?'

Fortunately, she didn't wait for a reply. 'Here's you snoring your head off in one room and Charley doing the same from his basket in the kitchen. Stereophonic snores were drifting up the stairs to assail my shell-like ears and disrupt concentration. I thought I'd better come down and investigate. When I spoke to the dog, he totally ignored me. Either because he was fast asleep or because he couldn't be bothered to make the effort to open his eyes. Males!'

With that she was gone and sighing, I heaved myself out of the chair and went to make the tea.

Chapter Five

With only 20 houses in the Close, a ritual had evolved over the years whereby those who were of age and able, congregated on high days and holidays for a nosh and knees up at somebody or other's house.

It began when both the houses and children of the early settlers were new and babysitters hard to come by. Having a party so near to hand meant both partners in turn could go. Nowadays we also had a bash early in June to which we magnanimously invited the children. It had in fact been at the last summer party when I finally emerged from my cocoon of self-pity.

Naturally, there were the odd dissenters who didn't approve of the neighbourly shindigs. Also times when one or other of the partners overstayed their allotted time span. Fortunately, the resulting domestic friction was usually short-lived, and on the whole, the system worked well. At the moment there were around eight couples who no longer needed babysitters so were able to spend the whole evening together whether they wanted to or not.

So, Jane and I made our way on Monday night to George Benson's house and as usual crawled home around three the following morning – fortunately not having far to crawl.

It was during the early part of the evening before the men were routed from the kitchen, there occurred one of those coincidences or twists of fate one reads about in novels, but very rarely meets in real life.

I was leaning against the sink listening to Dave Windsor, a fireman, talking about a call they'd dealt with during the early hours of that morning.

'Really bizarre it was,' said Dave. 'We laughed all the way back to the station.'

'Was it a fire?' someone asked.

'Oh no, nothing as serious as that. This was some idiot who'd got himself stuck and couldn't get free. It's usually kids or animals who get heads and fingers stuck or jammed, but this was a lad of around 19 or 20.'

'What happened?' I queried. We were all ears for Dave has a way with tales.

'I've been on nights all over the holidays and last night was my final spell of duty for a week. I was due to knock-off at seven, but this call came in about six. Emergency at a shop in Briscoe Street. The telephonist got this garbled message about a leg being caught in some floorboards and not being able to get it free.'

Dave paused and handed his empty glass to George for a refill, who said, 'Briscoe Street! Isn't that the trading area used a lot by the Greek community?'

Before replying, Dave took several swigs from his refilled pint. 'Yeah. You're not kidding. When we arrived, there was an almighty row going on between two very belligerent Greek women. Very glamorous they were in curlers and dressing gowns. And the lad whose leg was dangling through the ceiling was also yelling fit to beat the band in a mixture of Greek and English. The racket was unbelievable. What with the racket from him because he thought we'd have to saw through his leg, the moaning from his mate and the two women going at it hammer and tongs, it was sheer bedlam.'

'How did he get his leg stuck in the first place?' I ventured as several alarm bells clanged away in my head.

'Well, it seems the lad lived in the flat over the shop, both owned by his mother. The shop, a newsagent's, was leased to someone else, one of the screeching women as it happened – the other one being his mother. The lad and his mate decided to break into the shop and thought in their wisdom that a novel way of doing it would be to lift the floorboards in the flat and then remove the ceiling tiles into the shop. A simple matter. No hassle. They'd take what they wanted, replace the tiles and no one would be any the wiser.

'It didn't quite work out because as they were taking up the floorboards, the Greek lad's foot slipped and went straight through the ceiling of the shop. His leg was caught when the split lathes sprang back around his calf.'

'How do you know they were breaking into the shop?' Old Fred asked enunciating his words very carefully, having started on the pop very early. He was also propping himself up against the kitchen door for some stability.

'Because,' replied Dave, 'just a sec, Fred, I need another beer, it's thirsty work this tale-telling. Thanks, George. Where was I up to? How'd we know about the proposed break-in? Because the lad's mate, Billy, was sitting on the floor in the flat when we went upstairs. He was rocking back and forth, repeating over and over like a bloody mantra that it wasn't a good idea to break into the shop that way. When he wasn't moaning, he was giggling. Weird he was. They were both as high as kites.

'The noise was incredible from both the shop and the flat. There was the lad yelling he didn't want his leg sawn off, his mate moaning and giggling inanely, and the two women screeching like Liverpool fishwives.

'It didn't take long to release his leg once we were able to get started. He had to be reassured I don't know how many times that we wouldn't be sawing through his leg; though by this time the temptation was very great.'

'So, where's he now?' I questioned, hoping my voice sounded calmer than I felt. Looking down at the hand holding my drink, I was surprised to see it was as steady as a rock. I must be getting used to this life of outward deceit although my insides were rotating like so much butter in a churn. My bête noire had turned up again. 'Is he in hospital or gaol?'

'Neither,' replied Dave. 'Though by the time we'd managed to release him, the police and ambulance had arrived. The two women had obviously come to some sort of arrangement for neither lad was charged, and the injured one wouldn't go to hospital for a check-up. The leg wasn't broken only badly bruised and scratched, looked worse than it was. We told him to have a tetanus jab as a precaution, but he wasn't having any of that either and got even more abusive than before if that was possible. Not a nice character in any shape or form. Then his mother kicked off again only this time it was for her poor baby. At least that's what we thought she was on about. She was still as noisy but in a different key. Ships wouldn't need foghorns with her around. The fog would disappear in fright once she got started.

'The lad then turned on her, swearing in a mixture of English and Greek and she took it all. A complete about-face from the way she'd been yelling and screaming at the other woman a short time earlier – like a tigress protecting its cub. But if one of my sons spoke to anyone, never mind their mother, the way that lad spoke to her, they'd know what for. He's one despicable little toad.'

You're so right there, Dave, I thought, *and his mate's no better.* I sighed inwardly. Was this fate drawing me closer into their sordid lives, or was I reading more into it when it was only coincidence? But a New Year's Eve party wasn't the time or place to deliberate on coincidences or the hand of fate. To prove my point, at this juncture, Elaine Benson shoved her head around the door and shooed us all out of the kitchen to join the rest of the party.

As predicted, New Year's Day was spent very, very quietly both of us a shade under the weather. Or as my wife politely put it, I looked rough whereas she was merely rather delicate

The Close too was quiet all day, even the children weren't much in evidence. I did catch a glimpse of Old Fred striding down the road looking as bright as a button, not a bit like the man who'd spent the night on the Bensons' couch so drunk his wife commented there was no point in even attempting to get him home. All I can say is he must have the constitution of an ox. I didn't have a fraction of what Fred drank, and I felt wretched.

So, Jane did no illustrating, and I did no thinking. She spent most of the day sprawled on the couch, and I slumped in an armchair in front of the television watching mostly repeats but too lethargic to switch off. Cooking wasn't on the agenda either. When we felt like eating, I toasted the sandwiches I'd left in the fridge. I wonder if that could be construed as forward planning! We went to bed early, and Charley didn't get so much as a walk to the end of the path. Not that he seemed bothered, I think he was still recovering from his Fromlington Park experience.

Wednesday morning saw us up bright and early with Jane hard at work by eight. After washing up the breakfast things, I took myself off to the office and was soon sitting at my desk reading Sam's fax. I was so engrossed, I visibly jumped when the telephone rang, jangling shrilly in the deserted building. Grabbing it quickly to shut off the noise my 'Hello' came out as a strangled squeak.

'Hello. Tom?'

'Yes.' A familiar voice but one I couldn't recognise off-hand.

'Good. I wasn't really expecting anyone to be there but thought I'd try before ringing your home. This is Greg Mathieson by the way. Happy New Year to you.'

'Thanks, Greg. Same to you. Hope mine turns out better than the last one.'

'Indeed. How're you keeping these days?'

'Not too bad, thanks. Now you didn't ring just to wish me a Happy New Year and ask after my health. If I know you there's bound to be an ulterior motive.'

Greg laughed. 'You're dead right there. I've got a problem, a very urgent matter. Any chance of popping down to see me? Yesterday if you can.'

'What sort of problem?'

'It's too long and complicated to explain over the phone, but you'll no doubt surmise it's to do with a machine. It's really urgent.'

'I'm intrigued. I'll come now if you like, I've an hour or two to spare.'

'Good. I thought you'd be curious. We're not in the same place, by the way, we've got one of those units down on the docks. New Quay Industries, Mulberry Dock area. D'you know it?'

'I used to know the docks pretty well at one time. I did a lot of fishing there as a lad, but it's been years since I was last down that way. Is the layout still the same?'

'Yeah, pretty well. If you take the first left after you come off the third bridge, we're the fourth unit down. You can't miss us, but just in case I'll wait outside for you.'

'OK, Greg. See you in about 15 minutes. Bye.'

Mindful of my promise, I rang Jane, leaving a message on the answerphone to the effect that I was off to see yet another machine. Naturally, I didn't mention this one was genuine.

The docks hadn't changed since my days as a fishing-mad youth. Still the same four bridges, the same old warehouses and office buildings, the same grey, cold, choppy water. What had changed were the functions of those offices and warehouses. Renovated and smartened up they now went under the grand name of New Quay Industries, with openings for every type and size of business; except those for which the docks were originally built – shipping and everything connected with the maritime industry.

Today the Quays were deserted apart from a derelict hulk tied up on the far side of the dock, which caught my eye as I crossed the third bridge. Maybe that too would be utilised one day. A floating prison sprang to mind. Off the top of my head, I could nominate two petty villains to start off the inmate count.

Putting these fanciful thoughts aside, I pulled up beside Greg's car, which I noticed was the same old vintage Cortina he'd had for donkey's years. Getting out of my car, the wind cut through my jacket like a knife and I was glad to follow Greg into the deceptive warmth of the building. I say deceptive because it was hardly any warmer inside than out, but at least it was out of the biting wind.

'Glad to see you, Tom,' said Greg as he shook my hand. 'The machine's over here, we'll take a look at it and then nip cross to the cafe for a cuppa and discuss the problem where it's a bit warmer.'

Looking at the machine, I saw it was a Delta Mark IV. That was all that could be seen – the nameplate. The rest was either in cartons stacked against the back wall or laid out on the floor.

'Where on earth did you get this?' I asked. 'I didn't know MFI were into machinery, I thought they only dealt with household goods.'

'Hah. Very funny, but not very original. Everyone who comes in here says more or less the same thing.'

'What is it, a build your own machine by numbers? I sincerely hope you've got a drawing or two to go with it.'

"Oh yes indeedy, I made sure of them before I bid for the thing,' replied Greg extricating some rolled-up drawings from behind a carton. 'But come over to the cafe and I'll explain.'

Going out, the biting wind met us full blast. Shivering, I glanced round as Greg locked up. It really was a bleak, grey sight. Not another soul to be seen. Even the pigeons and seagulls had called it a day. Then I saw the cafe, away to the right of the L-shaped block of buildings, looking very much out of place with its green neon sign announcing "All Day Breakfast Bar" to an empty world.

'Its official name might be the All Day Breakfast Bar,' commented Greg as we walked towards the cafe. 'But to the folk round here it's commonly known as "Fat Freddie's" for more reasons than one. He does a mean line in fry-ups, believe me.'

'I'm surprised he's open today.'

'Fat Freddie is open every day from seven in the morning to midnight with the exception of, I think, Christmas Day. Mind you the night-time clientele aren't the same as the daytime lot.'

On this enigmatic note, Greg opened the door, the heat hitting us like a sauna as we went in. Probably a slight exaggeration but that's how it felt after the cutting wind and the ice floe that passed for Greg's workshop.

'D'you want any toast?' asked Greg handing me the roll of drawings and making his way towards the counter. Nodding I looked around for somewhere to sit and chose a table by a window overlooking the dock. The cafe was pretty busy, which surprised me a little until I reasoned that the place would be a haven for the lonely or an escape from the endless diet of festive food and television repeats.

Greg stopped at one such table on his way back to speak to its solitary individual, although judging from the look of this individual he wasn't escaping from too much food and television. He belonged to that army of down-and-outs who unfortunately are now part and parcel of urban life. When I was young, if we saw one tramp a year it was an occasion, and then it was usually during the summer months.

My thoughts along this vein were interrupted as Greg sat down and took off his jacket. Mine had already been thrown over the back of an empty chair, an indication of how warm it was in there. 'Friend of yours?' I asked.

'Old Dean Martin. One of life's dropouts. He comes in at least once a day. Someone will always buy him a breakfast, and if not, Big Marge makes sure he has at least one hot meal a day.' He smiled. 'He's not averse to three or four breakfasts if they're on offer. I don't know where he puts the food plus all the booze. There's hardly a pick on him under that sartorial elegance.'

In this instance, the sartorial elegance consisted of not the usual tattered military greatcoat, but an enormous astrakhan coat which had seen better days sometime in the last century, and which covered him almost from head to toe. I say almost, for I glimpsed a pair of highly polished army boots peeping from under the tattered hem of the coat.

I looked at Greg. 'Old Dean Martin?'

Greg started singing quietly, 'Little ole wine drinker me. Remember it? Old Dean over there's partial to wine in any shape or size of bottle, never drinks anything else, unless he can't get wine.'

'I couldn't help noticing the boots.'

'One of his little quirks. I suppose down-and-outs have quirks like the rest of us. Funny about Old Dean, he can be literally falling to bits everywhere else, but his boots are always highly polished, might not have any soles mind you, but you can always see your face in the uppers.' He glanced over at the man's feet. 'Father Christmas must've been, they look new. Probably Fat Freddie, that's where the coat originated from.' He rubbed his hands. 'Ah, here comes Marge.'

Carrying a large tray, Big Marge made her way towards us, stopping on the way to give Old Dean a piled-high plate and a steaming cup. 'Old Dean says thanks, Greg,' she said as she deposited our thick toast and strong tea on the table.

Greg looked over at him, and Old Dean waved a grimy hand in acknowledgement before tucking into his toast as if there was no tomorrow, which perhaps could well be, given his lifestyle.

Picking up a wedge of toast the size of a man's fist, I watched Big Marge make her way back to the counter and thought that weak tea and thin toast would never be part of her menu.

'Wait until you see Fat Freddie,' remarked Greg, aware of the expression on my face. 'Marge is anorexic compared to him. Now down to my little problem or problems.'

I laughed at him. 'How'd you come by your, as you mildly put it, little problem.'

'I'll start at the beginning. As you know, I manufacture small plastic tubs for butter, margarine and whatnot.' I nodded. 'Well, I've got an order that's got to be completed by the end of January. Now normally it wouldn't be a problem except my Delta finally gave up the ghost the week before Christmas. Fortunately, I'd heard on the grapevine about this Mark IV going under the hammer, so I took myself along to the auction and managed to get it quite cheap. Shame really, another firm biting the dust, but you know what they say about ill winds.'

Pausing, he bit into another toasted doorstep before continuing. 'What I wasn't prepared for was that it'd still be in its wrappings so to speak. The firm hadn't had time to assemble it before the receivers jumped in and everything came to a standstill. In one way this machine is the answer to my prayer, but in another I'm stymied by the time limit. As you know before I became a manufacturer, I was an engineer so I'm quite confident of getting the mechanics of the thing together but, and here's where I hope you fit in, I need an electrical engineer and you're the best I know. Time is of the essence as the saying goes. I reckon on two weeks for the actual manufacture of the tubs, so that leaves two weeks to construct the machine. I don't mind telling you, Tom, my business could hinge on this contract. A sign of the times, I suppose, so many small businesses lurching from one contract to the next. D'you think you'll be able to help?'

Picking up my mug I drank as I thought, the first one being that the tea was so strong it could be used to tar a flat roof. But back to Greg's problem. It wasn't so much a question of not wanting to help but more a matter of sorting out my own business affairs before going off to New Zealand. After a minute or two I came to the conclusion there wasn't any problem to consider. It would simply be a matter of condensing into four weeks what I was intending to do in six. I'd give the next fortnight to Greg and the following fortnight to my own affairs. It would also mean my amateur sleuthing would have to be put on hold. There'd be no time available for skulking or ferreting about. All my time and energy would be needed here helping Greg if the machine was to be up and running on time. Perhaps the enforced labour would banish all thoughts of detection from my mind. Perhaps put the hateful and painful episode into perspective as something unfortunate that had happened. A bad experience which was now over and done with. Perhaps. But I knew it wouldn't be so. I mightn't have time to dwell on the two B's, but deep down, I knew I couldn't put them completely out of my mind.

The whole episode had been like a sore tooth, constantly niggling in the background, flaring up every now and then to jolt me right back to that dreadful night and its aftermath. After my original sighting of the fair-haired youth, I knew my niggle would never go away until something was resolved. It suddenly dawned on me that while I'd been staring through the window thinking, Greg was still waiting for an answer.

'It's like this, Greg. Jane and I are off to New Zealand in a few weeks, Sam's getting married, sprang it on us the other night.'

Greg's face fell. 'Oh. Not that I'm not pleased, but it does throw any ideas of help out of the window, doesn't it?'

I held up my hand. 'Don't be too hasty. Of course, I'll give you a hand. I'll need a couple of weeks to sort things out with Jeff at my place before I take off; not that he knows anything about Sam's wedding or our trip yet. That'll be a little surprise for him when he gets back from Scotland. But I digress. I'll be able to give you a couple of weeks if that's any help, and as my place is closed until the ninth, I could even start tomorrow.

'Oh good,' sighed Greg. Relief written in large letters all over his face. He indicated the still rolled-up drawings. 'Have you time to look at these things now?'

We stayed in the cafe for another hour or two studying the drawings and discussing the machine, in between drinking Big Marge's thick brew.

Old Dean raised a dirty hand in farewell as we left, his pungent odour washing over us as we passed. It was hard to tell where the skin ended and the fingerless gloves began, both being the same shade of mouse-coloured grey.

'Don't worry,' said Greg as we hastily fastened our jackets having forgotten how cold it was after spending so long inside the warm cafe. 'That's Old Dean's regular table. When he's not there, Big Marge makes sure it's thoroughly disinfected, so you won't catch anything. Not unless it's something you want to catch,' he concluded.

On this slightly puzzling note, we said our goodbyes after arranging to start at eight the following morning, got into our cars and went our separate ways.

Chapter Six

Over lunch I regaled Jane with my morning's exploits, especially the visit to Fat Freddie's. 'If I go to that cafe too often, I'll soon be as big as Marge herself and Greg assures me that Freddie's even bigger. Can't wait to meet him.'

'Visible proof of their culinary arts no less?'

'And some. I've drunk so much tea this morning I should be swishing inside. But it was so thick and strong I think it's just sitting there in one big black lump.'

'Sounds vile. I presume you don't want any tea from this pot then?' said Jane as she filled her cup.

'No. I'll make myself a coffee in a sec, you can have the whole pot to yourself.'

'How long will this machine take to build?'

'Definitely all of this week and most of next I should imagine,' I called from the kitchen as I waited for the kettle to boil. 'So, my love, I'll be out of your hair for a while. After my labours for Greg, I'll need all the time that's left for my own stuff, which should ease your mind regarding yours truly being left on his own. Having, as you so quaintly put it, "time to brood".'

Taking my coffee back into the dining room I continued, 'This Heath Robinson machine of Greg's is going to take all the hours God sends and more if it's to be ready on time.'

Smiling slightly, Jane said, 'I keep telling myself I'm being silly, that lightning isn't supposed to strike twice in the same place. But I can't help it, Tom. That little bit of apprehension's always there, especially when you're out longer than expected.' Her long-fingered mobile hands were being used to good effect to emphasise her feelings. She sighed. 'I'm sorry, love, you can do without worrying about me worrying about you. That's not going to help either of us. I think this holiday is just what we both need.'

She was silent for a moment, mulling something over in her mind, and when she spoke, it was with conviction. A decision had been reached. 'I should be finished by this Sunday. So how d'you feel about going to Manchester on Monday? Make a day of it. We can call at Wilf's first to drop my stuff off, if anything needs altering, he can get them back to me during the week. Then we could go to the travel agents, book the flights, sort out visas and whatever else we'll need. Good job our passports are still valid for another few years. We'll have to pop into the bank to arrange our holiday finances, travellers' cheques and currency. I suppose we could both do with a new suitcase. Do you want to stop over on the outward journey? I don't. I'd prefer to wait until we're together on the way home. What about a wedding present? Any ideas? Did Sam mention anything about presents in her fax? People are bound to ask. Talking of faxes, where is it, how could I forget that? My mind's jumping from one thing to another.'

'So's your tongue. If your pencil moves as fast, you'll have your work finished by tomorrow never mind Sunday.' Laughing, I pulled the crumpled letter from my jacket pocket and passed it over.

Jane read it through quickly once, and then more slowly a second time. 'Hmm,' she said. 'No mention of presents. Did you send a reply?'

I shook my head. 'No. Greg phoned as I was reading that, and I more or less went off straight away to meet him.'

'Could you send one before you go to Greg's tomorrow? It need only be a few lines. We'll send a longer one when we know the travel arrangements and whatnot.' Jane looked at me and smiled. 'Another little thought's just crossed my mind, oh devious husband of mine. If you're going to be out all hours, doesn't that put paid to your offer of chief cook and bottle washer? Very convenient.'

I grinned at her. 'Yep, the kitchen maid deal's off. From tomorrow anyway.'

Jane held up her hand. 'Ah, but to prove you were sincere in your offer you can still be chief dog walker.'

'It looks like the rain'll keep off for a while longer,' I commented looking through the window. 'So, Charley and yours truly will stagger round the park, and this evening I'll prepare a gourmet meal the likes of which you've not had for a long time.'

'Egg and chips? You're right. We've not had that for months.'

'Cheeky madam. Get off with you and sharpen your pencils. Come on Charley, time for our penance round the park.'

Walking round the park, the local one this time, I tried to concentrate my mind on the logistics of building Greg's machine in the short time available to us. But Dave Windsor's New Year's Eve tale kept intruding. In the end, I gave it my whole attention as we ambled down paths, across grass and up and down the small hills that dotted the park.

So, Tom, I said to myself, you now know where they both live (that the lad with the injured leg was Bobby I was certain). But what purpose does knowing that bit of information serve? Not much really. It was simply another piece of the jigsaw I was putting together regarding my double bugbear. How many pieces would be in that jigsaw, or what sort of picture it'd make when the final piece was placed in position was a matter I wasn't dwelling on. No doubt I'd reach a satisfactory answer in the fullness of time.

After our gourmet meal of egg, chips and a bottle of wine followed by a dream-free night, I was down at the Quays almost before daylight next morning. I'd popped into my office on the way and spent about 15 minutes sending the fax to Sam which, as Jane had promised, wasn't very long plus a line or two of my own to the effect that I was looking forward to seeing her and sending her my love.

So here we were on this cold, bleak Thursday morning contemplating the seemingly mammoth task before us. It was barely light, and the intense cold of the workshop wasn't very conducive to taking off my thick winter jacket. Greg did have a portable heater, but it'd be quite a while before we'd feel any effects from that.

'I've asked my Boy Friday if he'll lend a hand,' said Greg with a grimace, taking off his jacket and donning a pair of freezing cold overalls, so stiff they could almost stand up by themselves. I'd come prepared and already wore overalls under my jacket so didn't have to go through the extra torture of thawing them out, just taking off my jacket was bad enough. 'Who's your Boy Friday, one of your lads?'

'Yes and no. I employ him high days, holidays and any time in between. He's 17, doing "A" levels at the local sixth form college. Comes when he can. I don't fit him in, he fits me in amongst all his other activities. Very grateful for small mercies. He's worth his weight in pots of tea. I'd employ him full time tomorrow, but he's got his sights set on higher things has young Jim. Anyway, he's coming in all this week and whenever possible after that to give us a hand.' Greg paused and watched his exhaled breath almost solidify into icicles, before saying, 'Especially where making tea is concerned. We'd have had at least two mugs by now if he was here.'

'Right, I can take a hint as well as the next man,' I said and went off to sort out the kettle and mugs. 'Is there any milk?'

'No. We get it from the cafe. Ah here's Jim now, he'll go for it. D'you want anything to eat yet?'

'No thanks.'

'Morning,' said a voice at my elbow a few minutes later. 'I'm Jim, here's the milk.'

I finished pouring the water into a teapot, which naturally was of the same vintage as the archaic heating, took the milk and looked at Jim. I don't know what I was expecting. A brawny six-footer? Teenagers seemed so tall these days. But Jim was about five and a half feet tall, slightly built, with bright red curly hair and freckles. Along with a cheerful face and a ready smile, he looked to be all of 14 years of age.

'Morning, Jim, I'm Tom. Where d'you keep the sugar?'

Preliminaries over, we got on with the immediate job in hand, namely pouring the tea and taking it through to the workshop. Greg grunting with exertion, was manoeuvring the base plates of the machine into position on the floor.

'This is about the only thing I recognise without having to look at the drawing,' he said, taking his mug of tea 'What d'you think'd be the best plan of action?'

'Well.' I look round the workshop. 'The drawings need to be somewhere accessible. I notice the cartons are all numbered, hopefully each one corresponds to the contents and numbers on this list. It might be a good idea though to leave the bits in their containers until we want them.'

'As I'm obviously the only technical one here I'll see to the drawings,' said Jim emerging from the office with a tin of drawing pins and proceeded to pin the sheets up on the wall, all the time whistling an old pop tune that was even familiar to me. Meanwhile, Greg and I got on with the labouring side of things.

Working steadily throughout the morning, fortified by numerous hot drinks, it must have been getting on for midday when we sat back and considered the drainage problem. The new machine was being positioned on the site of the old Delta which would pave the way for the adaptation of the existing facilities, such as the three-phase electricity supply, the lubricating oil sump, the pump and some of the feed pipes.

Greg looked at the relevant drawing pinned up on the wall and compared it to the old one of the Mark 1. This old drawing, rather faded and very creased, had been unearthed from his equally archaic filing cabinet. 'It's a miracle that was still there,' he said, 'I'm surprised it hadn't been chucked out ages ago.'

Jim and I exchanged glances. Miracle had nothing to do with it for even in the short time I'd been there it was obvious Greg was very reluctant to throw anything away.

'That's fairly new compared to some things in that cabinet,' said Jim nodding towards the Mark 1 plan. 'I've come across the original plans for Noah's Ark in there, complete with manifesto and bills of lading.'

He went off whistling "The animals went in two by two" as Greg laughed but forbore to comment. Instead, turning back to the matter in hand he said, 'With a couple of slight modifications we should be able to use the same drain. Just need about two feet of extra piping. That'll be one load off my mind. I was a bit worried the whole drainage system would be totally different. Instead, it should save us a whole day of extra work.'

'And, no doubt, also save me from having to go down said drain,' muttered Jim coming back from the cafe with several sandwiches the size of doorsteps. 'Docker's butty, anyone?'

'I'm surprised he knows what a docker's butty is,' I mentioned to Greg as Jim went to make the tea.

'It's his granddad,' was the only reply I got by way of an explanation. 'Now where's the nearest DIY centre?'

I looked at the list in my hand. 'The big DIY stores may be open, Greg, but they won't have the equipment we need. Gerragh's is about the only plumbers' merchant who'll be open, so we'll be OK for the pipework. But as for the electrical gear we're going to have to bastardise the stuff from the old machine. We'll look at that when I get back.'

'Shit,' said Greg. 'No wonder this country's going to the dogs. Why it's necessary to have such long Christmas breaks is beyond me.'

Looking at each other, Jim and I burst out laughing, and Greg had the grace to look sheepish when he realised what he'd said.

Leaving the workshop and walking towards my car, I looked towards the dock and shivered as the keen wind blew across the back of my neck. Pulling my collar up a little further, I watched the whitecaps, or rather greycaps, for a moment as they danced across the murky water. Glancing round, I ruminated on the bleak and empty quay and then smiled to myself. What did I expect? Parasols and windsurfing? It was early January after all. Not that I could imagine sun umbrellas and windsurfing on these quays at any time.

Driving past Fat Freddie's flashing neon sign, I mused anew on the incongruity of such a vivid sign in such an empty and derelict spot. However, catching a glimpse of a shambling figure in an enormous astrakhan coat, I realised that although the docks may appear empty, there was indeed life around, even if that life could be classed by some as being as empty and as derelict as the deserted docks themselves.

Chapter Seven

Crossing the four bridges, I reached the junction and turned right on to the main road. Gerragh's plumbing business was on the other side of town about four miles away and I could have turned either way. But by turning right, my journey would take me through the area where Bobby lived. Namely Briscoe Street. I don't know whether this was a subconscious decision or whether I was deliberately looking for another piece of the jigsaw. There was no ready answer. Not even to the question of why?

On reaching Briscoe Street, I drove about halfway down before stopping outside a newsagent's. Getting out of the car, I glanced at the upstairs windows, with the firm conviction that this was where Bobby had his flat.

Entering the shop, I stood unnoticed for a minute or two by the woman behind the counter. She was busy talking in Greek with great volubility, gesticulating as fast as she talked, to two other women. All three had their gazes turned towards the ceiling.

I too looked up at the newly replaced tiles and again felt loathing towards the youths, in stark contrast to the joviality with which I'd listened to Dave's story on New Year's Eve. But there I'd been in convivial surroundings, in the company of friends and close to home; far removed from Billy and Bobby's actual presence. It was disconcerting to feel like this here. Why should a few ceiling tiles have this effect on me?

'Yes.'

I dragged my gaze down from the tell-tale squares above my head to the woman behind the counter (now minus curlers and dressing gown) who'd finally noticed the stranger in her shop and automatically switched to English.

'Twenty Benson and Hedges please.' Placing the money on the counter I looked up at the ceiling venturing a comment on the newly replaced tiles. 'Burst pipe?'

'You could say that,' was her only reply as she gave me my change. Before I'd even left the shop, she was back with her cronies, their contemplation of the ceiling and the continuation of her tale, which was to put it mildly, all Greek to me.

Sitting in my car, I lit a cigarette and opened the window before driving off and wishing with all my heart it had been Bobby's neck caught in that ceiling, rather than his leg. I reflected I hadn't felt this anger when I'd visited Billy's home or when I'd passed them both in the street and wondered why!

'Stop trying to analyse your reasons and motives, Tom,' I said out loud. 'When you've reached a conclusion in whatever form then, if you want to, by all means pick through the whys and wherefores. In the meantime, get down to Gerragh's for that piping.'

Stopping at the traffic lights, I glanced over at the car next to me in time to see the driver who'd apparently been staring at me, shake his head in bewilderment and look away. Oh well, I smiled to myself. It's probably a good job he couldn't hear what I'd been saying otherwise he'd have been even more bewildered.

Fortunately, Gerragh's had the necessary piping and it wasn't long before I was on my way back to the Quays, taking the other route this time and turning my thoughts to Greg's machine and its attendant problems, rather than my own ever-circling speculations.

By mid-evening we were feeling very pleased with ourselves having managed to connect the relevant pipes to the appropriate taps without too much hassle and very little swearing. But as we were congratulating ourselves on the way we'd bastardised the old switchgear, trunking and conduit from the old machine, we hit the inevitable snag.

Sitting back on my heels I looked at Jim who, because we didn't have the right tools for the job, was busy sawing away with a hacksaw at a piece of conduit for which, of course, we were waiting. 'We could do that a lot quicker with a jigsaw,' I commented.

'You mean I could,' said Jim straightening up. 'I seem to have been hacking away at this piece for hours and getting nowhere fast.'

'Sod's law isn't it? In my eagerness to get started, I didn't think to check the tools. And naturally the jigsaw's one of those I took home for that bit of DIY.' Greg sighed as he pulled on his jacket. 'It'll take me the best part of an hour, so why don't you grab something to eat while you can. I'll snatch a sandwich at home.' He opened the door. 'Just look at that rain. See you soon.'

'I'll volunteer to get wet,' quipped Jim snatching up his coat and followed Greg through the door.

The rain was belting down, hitting the roof like tumbling stair rods, with the intermittent gusts of wind rattling the windows and door, as if it too wanted shelter. I thought of Old Dean Martin, wondering if he had somewhere dry to spend the night and pondered briefly on how he'd come to such a sorry state on his journey through life. Perhaps he didn't see it as a sorry state, it may have been preferable to the life he'd had. Who was I to say!

'You're theorising and philosophising again, Tom,' I said to the empty workshop. 'Get on and make the tea. And stop talking out loud to yourself as well. It's getting to be a habit.'

Off I went to make the tea, and by the time Jim was blown back through the door, I had it poured, and was sitting on the floor on some cardboard, with my feet straight out towards the central heating system. Greg's one-bar electric fire so old as to be undatable, but at least it still worked.

Jim had brought four hot pies. 'Too bad about my cholesterol level,' I said to him, 'but I'm going to enjoy these.' I was halfway through my second pie before I noticed Jim was only nibbling at his first. He was also very quiet, which was most unusual for him. He'd been full of his usual quips before he'd gone to the cafe.

'You're very quiet, Jim. Did something happen at Freddie's? It's not like you to pick at food.'

'No, nothing happened as such. But I saw Silly Billy in the cafe and that always upsets me.'

I stopped eating. 'Silly Billy?'

'Yeah. That's what he was called in school because of that silly laugh of his.'

Keep calm, I said to myself. *It mightn't be the same person.* But instinct told me it was the fair-haired lad Jim was talking about. I gave a quiet sigh. Another coincidence! Or the hand of fate? Whatever, it was a further strand to the web. I found myself gripping my mug so tightly my knuckles were white, and I was oblivious to the boiling hot liquid burning my palms through the cup. Only when I put the mug down did I noticed how red they were.

'Why does he upset you?'

Jim didn't answer my question directly. Maybe he hadn't heard me. Instead he carried on from wherever his thoughts had taken him.

'I learned karate because of him. My grandad said it wouldn't do any good bottling it all up. It wouldn't solve anything. In the long run, I'd only be hurting myself and him and Mum. I was only 11, too young to do anything constructive and nothing would bring Mark back, so he packed me off to karate lessons where I'—here Jim's voice changed to a monotonous reading by rote tone—'learned to control my anger and aggression and channel it elsewhere, as the jargon goes.'

'Who is Mark and what happened?'

'We'd been friends since we were little. We went to the same playgroup, then through infants and primary school. He was a very clever lad, academically brilliant but with very little common sense as some brainy people are. He was also very gullible, and I sort of looked after him, kept my eye on him and made sure he didn't make too much of a fool of himself. Well, in the summer holidays after we left primary school and before I was due to go to Newton Comp, I was in America at my dad's and Mark died from sniffing glue. It was the first time he'd ever done anything like that, but once was too much. He suffered from asthma and the fumes caused an attack, and he was dead before anyone could get help. He was only 11 and my best friend.'

Jim paused and took a gulp of tea. His pies, uneaten, were slowly congealing on the floor beside him.

'What does this so-called Silly Billy have to do with it?'

'Well, no one could or would say where Mark got the idea that it'd be OK to sniff glue. I told you he had no sense at times. Also, he was on his own when it happened. Everyone, his mum, dad, the police and so on just assumed that it was something he'd decided to try for himself just to see what all the fuss was about. It was all over by the time I came home; I didn't know until then. Mum, Grandad and my dad thought it'd be better that way, they didn't want to spoil my holiday. Anyway, when I went to Newton Comp in the September, Silly Billy and his mate, the Greasy Dago, were in the fifth form – not that they were there very often and they never came back after the Christmas holiday. I think the whole school heaved a collective sigh of relief. I didn't know much about either of them when I first went there except that they were odd, cruel and vicious. Billy's got this silly giggle and a funny walk; he skips every so often, and his greasy mate was best given a very wide berth.' I was in the cloakroom one afternoon when the pair came in for a sly smoke knowing it'd be empty that time of the day. Fortunately, they didn't see me because as soon as I heard them, I hid behind an old coat, which looked as though it'd been there since the school opened and smelt like it as well.'

He smiled and pointing at Greg's ancient heating contraption a touch of the usual happy lad emerged as he said, 'After seeing that and Greg's other antiques around this place, that coat would've felt right at home hanging behind a door here.'

His face sombre once more, he continued with his tale. 'Being much smaller than I am now.' I raised my eyebrows but made no comment. 'I was well hidden but hoped they wouldn't be long as I was getting a bit agitated about being out of class for so long. So, I was only listening to them with half an ear, expecting the door to open any minute and someone to call my name. Then I caught on to what they were saying and forgot about the door, the lessons, everything.'

Jim stopped and took a mouthful of tea. 'Ugh. That's freezing.'

'I'll make another one in a minute. Knowing Greg, he'll want one as soon as he gets back.'

'Yeah,' said Jim sighing and sat looking into space deep in thought.

In the short silence that followed I could hear the wind which had risen to gale proportions whistling around the building, while the rain still hammered on the roof, and once again thought briefly of Old Dean Martin. I don't know for how long that noise had been going on but so engrossed had I been in Jim's story that neither the gale nor the rain had penetrated my subconscious until now.

'One of those two bastards, I don't know which,' said Jim carrying on with his tale as if there'd been no interruption, 'said it was a pity about that kid in the holidays dying after the first sniff. I knew he meant Mark. The other said that it'd only been a little can at that. Silly Billy then said, and I quote word for word because they're burnt on my memory, "Who cares anyway, it's one snivelling little git less on the planet. No one'll miss him. But I'd have liked to have seen his face turn purple when he tried to get his breath. I've never seen anyone die." Then he went off into a fit of those awful giggles. I don't know how long it was after that before they left the cloakroom. But there was no way I could go back into the classroom. I just took to my heels and ran home; left my coat, bag, everything.

Don't even remember getting home I just know Grandad found me. I couldn't stop crying and couldn't even tell him why, though he knew it must've had something to do with Mark. I hadn't cried at all up until then. Anyway, he rang school to let them know where I was, and I stayed off the rest of the week. It was half-term the week after so by the time I went back, no one commented on my sudden disappearance. The friends that knew didn't say anything and I didn't discuss it with anyone else.

'That afternoon I cried and cried until there was nothing left. Mum was getting worried, but Grandad said it was for the best, he said I'd been too calm by far. It was that night when Mum had gone to work, she's a nurse, that I finally told Grandad what had happened in the cloakroom and that we should do something about it. But he said who'd believe a little boy mourning the loss of his friend? Those two'd deny they were ever in that cloakroom. Mark was alone when he died. Officially no one knows where he got the solvent from, whether he picked it up, bought it, or someone gave it to him. He was just another statistic, a childhood experiment that went tragically wrong. There was just no way anything could be pinned on those two; but being only a kid, I couldn't see why it wasn't straightforward. It was black and white. I'd heard them say they'd given Mark the solvent, therefore they'd murdered him. No problem.

'It was a long time before Grandad finally got through to me that life wasn't straightforward, in fact it had a habit of seeming to favour the ungodly. I grew up a lot that night and I've never cried since. Anyway, Grandad said my feelings needed channelling, I needed to control my emotions over the matter so they wouldn't get the better of me, especially with going to the same school as them. That's why I took up karate which, along with my schoolwork and whatnot, took all my concentration and energy so I had no time for brooding and becoming "emotionally damaged" as the experts would say.'

Pausing he stretched his legs out towards the fire and flexed his arms before saying, 'Fortunately, I didn't come across them in school very often, and as I said they never came back after the Christmas holidays. I don't think they were old enough to leave but no one cared, especially the teachers; and the powers that be didn't seem bothered. I've only seen them once or twice since, and I'm always surprised that they're still alive and kicking because I've heard they're on the hard stuff now.' He grinned. 'Hopefully, either that or someone'll do for them before long. It's funny though, I've never seen them in the cafe before now. But then I'm not usually here at night. There's a different type of customer in there once it goes dark; perhaps that's why Fred runs the place at night. The police must know what goes on, maybe it's in their interest just to keep an eye on the place in the hope of bigger things. Those two are only small fry, they haven't got the brains for anything bigger. That sounds like Greg now. No, it's OK, I'll make the tea.'

With that, Jim got to his feet, collected the cups and cold pies and made for the office as Greg tried to close the door with his foot against the force of the wind.

I too heaved myself off the floor with a groan and attempted to put some life in my cold and stiff limbs as I went to give Greg a hand and relieve him of his burdens.

Chapter Eight

On Friday we only had the pleasure of Jim's company, hard work and humour, until about four in the afternoon. He was off to the Midlands to a pop concert, and we wouldn't see him again until late on Monday.

I volunteered to go over to the cafe that evening, driven not only by hunger but also by my metaphorical toothache. I hadn't slept much the previous night, tired though I was. Jim's story was going round and round in my mind, and when I eventually did drop off, I had nightmares about giant aerosol cans emitting silly giggles and skipping on and off pavements.

Throwing on my jacket, I headed for the cafe, weaving my way between the parked cars, surprised at how many there were, pushed open the door and went in.

For a moment, I thought I was in the wrong place.

During the day, the cafe was bright and cheery, with several tables set aside for non-smokers. Now the lights were so dim as to be practically non-existent, and the whole room was thick with smoke. There was also an impression that every table was occupied by huddles of two, three or four people. When my eyes eventually adjusted to the gloom and smoke, however, I saw that each huddle was positioned so as to be as far away from its neighbour as possible, and that empty chairs had been strategically placed for just this purpose.

I made my way to the counter behind which stood the largest man I had ever set eyes on. My initial impression was that he was as wide as he was tall. A slight exaggeration I admit but he stood well over six feet, filling the space behind the counter to capacity. He was also as bald as a coot.

Greg was right. Big Marge would definitely be sylphlike next to him.

'Evening, mate, what's it to be?'

'Four hot pies please.'

'Right. They'll be about five minutes. You Greg's mate helping him with that machine?'

'Yes, I'm Tom.'

'My name's Freddie. Known as Fat for obvious reasons.' He chuckled and several chins and other layers wobbled in unison threatening to turn his eyes into the merest slits. 'Where's young Jim tonight then? Hey cut that out.'

For all his bulk and weight, Freddie could move. He shot from behind the counter and crossed the floor before I'd realised his change in tone hadn't been addressed to me, but to some youths sitting at a table somewhere in the centre of the room. Freddie lifted both lads bodily from their chairs, one in each massive hand, and dragged them to the door, quickly opened by a helpful customer.

Propelling them through the opening, Freddie said, 'You know the rules of this establishment. Don't come back.'

With that he shut the door, turned and let his gaze sweep round the cafe, whereupon every head was once more bent in a huddle. Except mine. I stood there, to use the vernacular, gobsmacked at the speed which the incident had taken place. I didn't know either what (I use the term loosely) crime the youths had committed. Whatever it was, it must have been a heinous crime against the house rules and regulations.

'Sorry about that,' said Freddie returning to his side of the counter. 'Four pies, wasn't it? Did you say where young Jim was tonight?'

'He's gone to a pop concert in Birmingham, so we're doing our own gofering this weekend.'

'Good lad is young Jim,' called Freddie as he went into the kitchen.

Gathering he wasn't expecting an answer, I leant against the counter enjoying the warmth, notwithstanding the dim lights and smoky atmosphere. The whisper of voices from a nearby table floated across the gloom. I found myself intrigued and fascinated by the muted conversation, parts of which drifted across to me.

'We can only do this job when it's dark because that... ... most active.'

'... get the mole... and jemmy.'

'Need soft shoes, dark clobber and a balaclava.'

'... bash with a spade.'

'Don't forget the torch... long length of rope, lasso after bashing with the spade.'

All sorts of possibilities went flashing through my mind which, along with my imagination, shifted into overdrive. What sort of job was being planned? Violent, no doubt about that. I knew what it was like to be on the receiving end of a boot. But a spade! I shuddered and found it extremely hard not to turn round to try and pinpoint the prospective perpetrators.

I don't know what sort of expression was on my face for Freddie returned just then, looked at me oddly and said, 'They'll only be another couple of minutes, had a run on pies tonight.'

Hearing the sound of chairs being scraped along the floor as the occupants pushed them back from the table, Freddie's gaze shifted to my left. 'Night, George, Jem, Tony.'

A chorus of voices answered in unison. 'Night, Fred, see you tomorrow.'

A cold draught sent a shiver down my spine as the door opened and the men left the cafe.

'The boys are on nights at Borton's up the road,' Freddie enlightened me. 'Every time they come in here they've got a new strategy for getting rid of Jemmy's moles. He's plagued by them every spring. Through the winter plans are laid and re-laid with meticulous precision. They haven't caught a single one yet. Those pies should be ready by now.' He departed back into the kitchen, leaving me alone with my thoughts and a very red face.

A shrewd, canny man was Freddie. He knew I'd overheard George and his mates and made assumptions accordingly, the wrong ones as it turned out. But it was a salutary lesson to me not to tar everyone in the cafe with the same brush.

I could still hear voices from various parts of the room but very few words were distinguishable. With a wry grin I reasoned that if I was discussing any nefarious business, I too would be as quiet as the proverbial church mouse, not talking in a voice loud enough to alert every pimp, nark and snout in the place. I suddenly smiled. Pimp, nark and snout indeed. I must be reading too many penny dreadfuls, as my mother would say. Or the thick sulphurous air in the cafe had affected my reasoning to the extent I imagined myself to be in a den of iniquity. Yet another of my mother's moral epigrams.

I smiled again, this time at Freddie as he came out from the rear of the cafe. He grinned back but didn't say anything as he proceeded to wrap the pies and hand them over.

'That'll be one pound eighty. Ta. You should try some of Marge's soup, it's as hot and thick as an extra overcoat.' Handing me my change he smiled again. 'Night, Tom.'

Saying goodnight, I made my way towards the door still slightly bemused by the two incidents ostensibly similar in origin, to my overactive imagination at least, but totally different in reality, when pausing to let two men sidle past I heard Billy's silly laugh.

I didn't even have to turn my head to see him for he was at a table in an alcove behind the door, visible to anyone leaving the premises, but not on entering. As to be expected, he wasn't alone. Bobby sat next to him. Their backs were to the door and they sat opposite a third person. A seemingly nondescript little man, wrapped in a black overcoat and a voluminous scarf that threatened to strangle him any minute. There was, however, nothing nondescript about his voice. Stepping back once more to allow a third man to scuttle past, I heard him speak very quietly but very distinctly in a voice that chilled right through to the bone it was so cold, flat and final. I gave

an involuntary shudder even though the words hadn't even
been addressed to me.

'You don't deliver, you know the consequences. Thursday,
don't forget.'

The words were followed by Billy's inane giggle, which still
rang in my ears as I closed the door behind me and made my
way across the quay to the workshop.

With mixed emotions, I wended my way between the cars.
Emotions ranging from anger and rage that Billy and Bobby
should be sitting there free as birds. Chagrin for the way I'd
earlier jumped to the wrong conclusions, and a genuine fear
from the menace in the little man's voice.

I shivered. Someone walking over my grave! Or perhaps
just the cold night air after the warmth of the cafe! Whatever it
was, I was glad to close the door of the workshop behind me
and get down to the business of supper.

'Have I only been gone 15 minutes?' I asked Greg, looking
at the clock, another of his "antiques". 'It seems like hours.'

'What did you think of Freddie?' he mumbled from the
depths of a pie.

'Well for all his size he can't half shift.' I told him about the
incident regarding the youths. 'He must have eyes all round
his head, never mind front and back, and I still don't know
what house rules they'd broken.'

'Nothing gets past our Freddie that's for sure, it's probably
why he's managed to stay in business so long.'

'He certainly knew who I was and the assumptions I'd
made from bits of an overheard conversation.' I enlightened
Greg on the snatches of talk I'd heard from Jem and his mates,
and the fact that on hearsay alone I'd taken it for granted that
everyone in the cafe that evening had been up to no good.
'Freddie knew what I'd been thinking but passed no comment
about my moral judgements of his clientele. He just made me
feel very foolish.'

'I'd say there's about half of his night-time customers like
the three you heard, who pop in between shifts, or to and

from work. But the bulk of the remainder are definitely rogues and thieves.'

'What exactly goes on in there? All I could see when I eventually penetrated the smog were groups of men in huddles. There may've been women, but I wouldn't swear to it.'

Warming to his theme as well as his pie, Greg replied, 'Fences with clients, both sellers and buyers. Thieves arranging jobs and knock-offs. Drugs, petty or otherwise I should imagine. Usually it's a pub where you'd be offered things from the back of a lorry, but round here it's Freddie's cafe. Mind you this is pure supposition on my part. I could be wrong, but somehow, I don't think so. Would you take Jane there for a Saturday night cup of coffee after a romantic stroll along the docks? The answer's no on both counts. We just don't belong in that sort of environment.' He laughed as he drained his mug of tea. 'Unless of course you're after a new television or video, or perhaps a camcorder for your holiday, at a knock-down, or knock-off, price. It could also suit the law to leave a place like Freddie's alone most of the time, they know where to pick up their villains, petty or otherwise, when they need to.'

My villains hadn't been picked up, neither were they petty, not to me certainly and I don't suppose young Mark's family would consider his death a petty act. They were still around as large as life, doing their deals and unsolved muggings. I wondered how many other young lives had ended like Mark's because of them.

By my standards, my villains were definitely not petty. But who defined what was and wasn't petty? And that weird character they were with in the cafe certainly wasn't small fry. Recalling his voice, I felt the hairs rise on the nape of my neck.

'Right, back to work, I suppose.' Greg's voice jolted me back to the present and the job in hand. Once more, my niggling toothache had to take a back seat, as we again busied ourselves with our particular tasks.

It was later than usual when we left that night. There'd been a difficult piece of machinery we wanted to sort out rather than leave it until the next day, so it was almost midnight when we packed up.

'See you about 10 tomorrow,' Greg called getting into his car. 'I think we deserve a lie-in.'

I don't smoke when I'm working so always take time to light a cigarette before getting into my car at the end of the day. Drawing in deep lungfuls of smoke, I happened to glance up as Greg's car passed the last alleyway between the buildings. Caught in his lights as he swept past were two figures pressed against the wall. There was no mistaking them – Billy and Bobby. Bobby's leg obviously wasn't impeding his ability to get around for just then they came out of the alley and quickly made their way back towards the now darkened cafe.

They looked funny in a macabre sort of way, and if I hadn't known them, I'd have been genuinely amused. One was skipping and one had an exaggerated limp. Quite a regular vaudeville double act, but I doubted if they'd ever qualify for an Equity card.

The long hours I'd been working hadn't left very much time for thinking or brooding about the pair, apart from my nightmare and the occasional stab from my metaphorical toothache. But the fact that they'd turned up almost on my doorstep was one more reason – be it chance or destiny – why I couldn't put them totally out of my mind. Whether they were frequent callers at the cafe or these last two evenings had been random visits was something only time and observations would reveal.

Flicking the butt-end of my cigarette through the window, I realised how rigid I was. Taking a few deep breaths, I relaxed my shoulders and started the car. Putting all thoughts of Billy and Bobby from my mind, at least for the time being, I concentrated on negotiating the potholes and diversions on the main road and getting home in one piece.

Chapter Nine

'Open your eyes, Sleeping Beauty, it's a quarter to nine.'

Struggling up out of the depths of a deep sleep which thankfully, as far as I was aware, had been dreamless, I opened one eye, pushed myself up on the pillow and looked at Jane.

'To my recollection, Sleeping Beauty was awakened with a kiss,' I mumbled still befogged with sleep.

'So she was, but she'd been sleeping for a hundred years don't forget. But if that's what you want, my Prince, that's what you shall have.' With that Jane planted a quick kiss on my cheek and muttered, 'Mind you, I don't think Sleeping Beauty was in need of a shave.'

'Who said romance is dead,' I sighed rubbing my bristly face. 'But you're right about the shave, I was too tired last night; in fact, I could cheerfully emulate Sleeping Beauty and sleep for a hundred years.'

'Well, you've had your quota for this morning. Anyway, shouldn't you be at the workshop by now?'

'Late start today. Ten o'clock. Didn't I tell you last night?'

'You did mumble something when you got into bed, but for the life of me, I haven't a clue what it was. I was only aware of your freezing cold feet. How's the machine coming along by the way?'

'Pretty much on schedule, give or take the usual setbacks and problems one encounters when one (or three in this case) is building a work of art from scratch.'

Jane laughed. 'Don't be so smug and drink your tea before it gets cold. Greg does know you won't be there on Monday, doesn't he?'

'Oh yes, my love, he knows. I haven't forgotten either.'

'It's going to be a busy day. There's the travel agents, the shopping, and whatever else comes to mind. We've also got a lot to talk about. We don't seem to have had a proper conversation for days.'

'Yep. It does appear as if my life at the moment consists of anything and everything to do with machinery.' *But*, I said to myself, *my thoughts at times are far removed from the business of engineering. No time, however, to go down that road this morning.*

I returned my attention to Jane. 'How about your work, are you nearly done?'

'I should be finished sometime tomorrow morning. Then it'll just be a matter of getting everything in order and tidying up, which'll probably take another couple of hours. Hopefully, everything should be done and dusted by teatime. I'd suggest going out to eat, but I assume it'll be another late night for you. I take it you are working tomorrow?'

'Fraid so,' I replied, sipping my tea. 'But will your bone-weary husband be able to have a lie-in on Monday before he's dragged kicking and screaming round the shops?'

Jane laughed in derision. 'Bone weary! Don't make me laugh. Also, when was the last time you were dragged round any shops? Not in the last century to my knowledge. And no, you won't be able to have a lie-in because we've got to be at Wilf's for nine and you know it'll take at least an hour to get to Manchester. Monday morning on the motorway won't be any picnic. But to compensate for your lack of beauty sleep (not that it'd make any improvement in your case), I'll do breakfast. How's that for a compromise?'

With that parting shot, Jane left the bedroom, leaving me to finish my tea and stagger, still tired and weary, to the shower, which worked wonders on my body if not my mind.

After breakfast, I picked up my car keys and went into the kitchen to say goodbye to Jane whereupon the dog gazed at me in anticipation. As I shook my head, he looked at me accusingly, gave one of his huge martyred sighs before curling up in his basket and burying his head in disgust.

'Sorry, old boy, not today.' I patted his head which elicited no response whatsoever, so leaving him to his sulks, I gave Jane a quick hug and a kiss and went on my merry, or weary, way.

Driving along I recalled that it was on such a day as this, bright, crisp and cold, that Charley and I'd done our marathon around that blessed park and I'd had the whistle-stop tour of "Call me Brenda's" house. I cringed at the memory. I must have been mad, out of my tiny mind. What on earth possessed me to do such a thing I've no idea. I hated to think what Jane would say if she ever found out.

I was probably still a little mad. Now, however, it was a cold, calculated kind of madness, one which no one but me would ever know about. I would have my revenge on Billy and Bobby. When or how I didn't yet know, but the certainty was there. Mark too would be avenged, even though I'd never known the lad, never known he'd even existed until the other night. Jim's story had made a deep impression on me, not only for his loss but for the waste of a young life which had had so much potential. How much potential did the two B's have to offer? None. I must have driven on autopilot, for I arrived at Greg's place without any recollection of negotiating potholes or any other diversions on the way. Unless I'd become so used to them that I steered round them automatically. But still, it wasn't a good thing to be driving round with my mind so full other things that I was oblivious to all other traffic.

There was little point in having a post-mortem on my driving habits so locking the car I went into the workshop to get on with the reason I was there in the first place – the building of a machine.

Greg and I worked steadily throughout that day, fortified with countless mugs of tea. A half-hour break at lunchtime with yet more tea but this time we had sandwiches to mop up some of the liquid. Gradually the machine was beginning to take shape and resemble what it was supposed to be, rather than a series of unconnected bits of metal and wiring like some abstract sculpture of the type that attracts so much attention in galleries and the media.

Neither of us spoke much, being preoccupied with our own thoughts. Greg's almost certainly to do with the machine, whereas while my hands were busy with wiring and connecting, my thoughts kept straying elsewhere. Chiding myself did no good either. It wasn't as if I was doing any constructive thinking, I wasn't. All I was getting were mental pictures of Silly Billy and Bobby giggling and sniggering and of how much I'd like to throttle the pair of them.

'Shall I nip over to Freddie's? I think it's time we had a break.'

Greg's voice brought me back to reality and the conclusion, judging by the stiffness in my legs, that I'd not moved for quite a while and had obviously been staring into space. Looking at my watch I saw it was getting on for nine.

'Sorry, Greg, I was miles away there. No, I'll go, it'll get the stiffness out of my joints. D'you want to try some of Marge's soup which Freddie swears is as good as an extra overcoat – thick and hot.'

'OK. As long as it's not like Old Dean's astrakhan coat, black and hairy. Get a couple of rolls as well. Freddie'll give you a basin or something to carry the soup in. I'll do the honours with the kettle.'

I was back in no time and true to Freddie's boast the soup was good and warming. The cafe had been smokier and more crowded than the previous evening. Or so it seemed to me as I peered through the grey and brown haze that hovered like a miasma around the place, distorting not only the whisper of voices but also the shapes of the bodies huddling in their little groups around the tables. For a moment it looked quite surreal and menacing. The smoke wrapped itself around me, threatening to suck me into their sordid little world. For some reason, Dante's famous, or infamous words came to mind. "Abandon hope all ye who enter here." But then I saw Freddie's cheerful face behind the counter and sanity returned, for the time being anyway. My imagination had definitely been on overtime for a short while, and I was smearing everyone with the same rancid butter, which was perhaps a little unfair. What about my own vengeful thoughts! Wasn't the thought father to the deed?

This philosophising was brought to an end by Freddie handing me a large covered basin filled with soup, and after promising to return the basin, I made my way to the door and the cold, but fresh, air. On my way out, I noticed that my pet villains were at the same table with the same man – only this time no one was speaking. However, I caught out of the corner of my eye, the man in the scarf passing a packet over the table to Bobby, who slipped it out of sight so fast it left me wondering if I'd imagined it.

The journey across the car park in the bitter cold put any further wonderings right out of my mind, and the appetising smell of the soup made me realise just how hungry I was. It took only a few minutes before Greg and I were dunking bread into Marge's soup and relishing every mouthful.

It was during this short break that Greg mentioned my attack. 'Did they ever get the bloke who mugged you?'

'No. And there were two of them. The police apparently knew who they were but there wasn't enough proof. Both had cast-iron alibis. The mother of one of them swore blind they'd both spent that night at her house.'

Greg interrupted me. 'You know what some mothers are like about their sons.'

'Yeah. Blind, deaf and dumb to any or all their faults. It doesn't do the kids any good in the long run.'

I didn't enlighten Greg to the fact that I too knew who my attackers were, nor that they were sitting as large as life over in Freddie's cafe right this minute. I was becoming more secretive and devious as the days went by.

'It's funny isn't it,' continued Greg, 'how the meaning of words changes over the years. Now when I was a kid if you mugged someone, you gave them money. Now it means the exact opposite, you take it from them by force. I much prefer the old version.'

'Me too. It's far less painful for a start.'

'Are you fully recovered now?'

'Physically – no longer than it takes for ribs to knit and bruises to fade. But mentally – oh that was a very different matter.'

'Did you get any help?'

'Yeah, but I found at the end of it, no matter how much hand-holding, pill-popping, meaningful discussions or whatever else is on offer, the determination to get well has to come from inside the victim or sufferer. I eventually came to the conclusion that no one could help me but myself. My pride had taken a beating as well as my body, but I think it was also my pride that made me pull myself together again. I ultimately realised that by wallowing in misery and self-pity, the only ones getting hurt were myself and my family.

'The muggers weren't bothered. Why should they be? I was of no further interest to them; they'd got what they wanted and hadn't been caught. No doubt they'd gone on to victims or pastures new. So, it was down to number one to sort myself out. That's my theory anyway. But as I said it took a long time. I like to think I've fully recovered, but I still have the occasional nightmare and until starting on this job with you, was very hesitant about being out late on my own even in the car. That doesn't bother me any more I'm glad to say. Mind you I don't go to the club as often as I used to, and when I do, I always get a taxi home.'

Greg laughed. 'It's a good thing for me then, isn't it? They do say that it's an ill wind, don't they? Whoever *they* are.' He looked at the clock. 'Oh well, we've had all of 20 minutes, you can tell Jim's not here, he'd have had us back after 15. To the grindstone it is.'

I lumbered to my feet as he continued, 'If we manage to get that capacitor fitted tomorrow, I'll be able to work on the baffle plates on Monday when you're off gallivanting round Manchester. Hopefully, it'll be sorted out for Tuesday. I bet Jane's looking forward to seeing you for a few hours at one stretch.'

'I'm not looking forward to traipsing round the shops though.'

Greg slapped me on the back. 'Be a man, grin and bear it.' He looked at the machine, heaving a sigh that came up from the depths of his boots. 'Why, oh why, wasn't I born one of the idle rich instead of handsome and poor.'

I looked at his craggy lived-in face and roared laughing. 'Come on, Adonis, the sooner you get started the sooner we'll finish, and then you too can re-introduce yourself to your wife.'

As on the previous night, it was almost midnight when we left the workshop. The usual cold wind was blowing across the dock, and I shivered involuntarily. Someone was again walking over my grave, or I was colder than usual.

Across the Quay, I could see Fat Freddie getting into his Mercedes, waving as he drove by. There's plenty of money in grease and fat I thought, but it needs to be the right kind of grease. Lighting my usual cigarette, I got into my modest Saab, and following Greg's rear lights left the dock. Not before, however, I glanced into the last alley on the left and there as on the previous night were the cause of all my nightmares. Billy and Bobby. 'I know whose graves I'd like to walk over,' I muttered to the freezing air streaming through the open window.

It seemed at least that some sort of pattern was beginning to emerge regarding their habits, at least for Thursday, Friday and Saturday evenings. Did it apply to the rest of the week as well I wondered? No doubt I'd find out tomorrow evening.

In the meantime – home. A hot drink, preferably laced with something purely medicinal, and bed was the order of the day or rather the night. So, with these thoughts in mind, I turned the corner and headed for home.

Chapter Ten

We packed up early on Sunday night. It was around nine and we'd reached a stage where carrying on would have meant we'd still be there in the wee small hours of Monday morning.

'I think that'll do for tonight,' said Greg wiping his oil-stained hands on a greasy rag fished out from his back pocket. 'Once we start fitting those funnels we'll have to stay until they're all done however long they take. Somehow I don't think Jane would thank me for sending a zombie round Manchester with her.'

I wouldn't thank you either for being said zombie,' I replied. 'Though on reflection, it mightn't be a bad idea. I hate shopping so much, perhaps I could sleep-walk my way round.'

Greg laughed. 'No, thank you. I'd hate to be on the receiving end of Jane's tongue if that happened. Come on, with a bit of luck I can be home by half-nine.'

'And fast asleep in the chair by a quarter to ten.'

He stripped off his overalls and pulled on his jacket. 'You're probably right there, but at least Kate'll have a face to look at for a change, even one in repose. See you Tuesday. Enjoy your day.'

Jane was surprised and delighted when I arrived home some three hours earlier than usual. Giving me a hug and a kiss, she said, 'I gather you haven't eaten yet. How about a stir-fry or would you prefer egg and bacon?'

Resting my chin on her head, I held her close. 'We must meet like this more often,' I mumbled into her hair. 'Stir-fry will do fine, but a big decision has to be made here and now. Should I take Charley for a walk first or have a shower?'

'Such a momentous decision as that I'll leave to you. Mind you, you do smell a bit oily and greasy, but for all that it's nice that you're home early. What happened?'

'We'd reached a point where it was either go home or stay until the early hours, and Greg didn't think you'd welcome the latter. Neither did he think you'd appreciate a zombie trailing around Manchester with you.'

'Quite right.' She pulled away from me. 'I think your big decision's already been made for you – definitely a walk.'

'Hold on there, Charley,' I said as the dog pranced round my legs whining with excitement, while I attempted to fix his lead. 'I'm only taking you round the block, not on a marathon. It'll be a quick walk at that, I'm starving.'

By the time we returned, and I'd had my shower, supper was ready. I think the dog had been prepared for an extended walk and was quite disgruntled by his short run, making no bones about letting his feelings be known. Huffing and puffing, dragging on his lead and sighing but to no avail. I was hungry and I'd said a short walk, and a short walk was what he got.

He was still moaning in no uncertain manner even after our return, and he lay with his head on Jane's lap looking at me in disgust as I ate.

We were both laughing over his antics as I said, 'Is your work all done?'

'Yep. For a while there this afternoon I thought I'd never be finished, but it worked out in the end.'

'What happened, did you mess up a drawing?'

'No, I had an unexpected visitor. It was a bit annoying when the doorbell rang, I didn't want to be interrupted. I thought being Sunday it'd be Jehovah's Witnesses or somebody like that, but when I saw who it was, I didn't mind one bit.'

'Who?' I shoved another forkful of food into my mouth. 'This is good.'

'Ted Jarvis.'

I looked at Jane in surprise. 'The policeman?'

'The very same. He was in the area and thought he'd pop in to see how we were.'

'It must be at least six months if not more since we last saw him. How is he?'

Ted Jarvis was the policeman who'd kept in touch with Jane and me since the attack. He'd said several times the police were often frustrated by the ease with which some criminals appeared to get off with their crimes through a technical matter, a legal loophole or an unshakeable alibi.

I now knew who'd attacked me and the police had known for a long time that Silly Billy and Bobby were the culprits but had been unable to bring a charge, because of the watertight alibi given by Bobby's mother. She'd lied through her teeth for those two vermin, but she wasn't doing them any favours in the long run. They'd trip up eventually.

Jane continued, interrupting my train of thought. 'Ted's been assigned to a new post. Community policeman and schools liaison officer. He said he's kept very busy but is enjoying the challenge and it's quite rewarding. They're even making some headway with "certain elements of the youth population in the area" – his words not mine.'

'What area's that?'

'It's an area I don't know, only by repute, well the name of the park anyway. Fromlington Park, which Ted says is the centre of his beat.'

I almost choked on my meal and took a sip of water to cover my shock. *My God*, I thought. *Another coincidence! Another strand in the web!* This news certainly puts paid to any latent ideas for revisiting that park ever again. I went cold at the prospect of what excuses or lies I would've produced, like rabbits from a hat, if I'd bumped into Ted last Sunday. Excuses and lies wouldn't have worked anyway for Ted would obviously know that at least one of my assailants lived in the area and would quite rightly surmise that I also knew.

Perhaps I'd been seen, and he'd called today for an informal chat on the matter. But by the same criteria, Jane would also know? The sweat stood out on my forehead and surreptitiously wiping my brow I stole a quick glance, but she was looking down at the dog and absently playing with his ears. 'Damn good job that dog can't talk,' I muttered under my breath.

'Stir-fry too hot?' said Jane looking up.

I gave her a wide grin. 'Nothing gets past you does it, my lovely?' I wiped my forehead again, openly this time.

Jane grinned back at me. 'I wondered how long it'd take before the peppers got to you.'

The peppers and your news both, combining to give me apoplexy, I said to myself, not even attempting to mutter one single word. I'd had enough frights for one day.

'Did Ted stay long?'

'About half an hour. We had a cup of coffee and I told him our news. Where you were, what you were doing, Sam's wedding and our trip.'

'So, the poor man didn't manage to say much at all.'

'Don't be cheeky. He talked for quite a while about his job, he's full of enthusiasm and optimistic about it. He's been in that area for three months now, and as I said he's pleased at the progress he's made. He did admit though that there's a small segment they'll never get through to. They just don't want to listen to anyone or anything that smacks of authority, no matter how benign.'

'How did you say you knew the area?'

'I didn't. Only by reputation and what I've read in the local papers. There's been quite a bit recently about the area becoming a thriving habitat for young villains, and people were going round in fear for the safety of themselves and their belongings. But you don't believe all you read in the papers do you. Miriam Walsh's family live round there, and she says it's much like any other inner-city region with high unemployment. A mixture of good and bad. It's nowhere near as bad as the papers make out. Miriam's family are quite happy to carry on living there.'

'Who's Miriam when she's at home?'

'Oh, Tom, you know her. She works at the greengrocers on Church Road. The big girl with red hair, the one who says she fancies you something rotten.'

'Oh, is that her name. Well, I won't be going for the spuds in future, I'll be too embarrassed.'

'Don't talk rubbish, you know you lap it up.' Looking down, Jane fondled the dog's head as she said, 'Do you know Fromlington Park?'

All sorts of questions flashed through my mind. Was this an innocent question? Had Ted noticed me in the park? Had he told Jane and was she gently probing?

I'm definitely not cut out for this life of subterfuge and deceit. In order to be a good liar, a person not only needed a good memory but also the ability to think fast and come up with convincing answers.

I decided to tell the truth with only one little white lie. 'If it's the Fromlington Park in the north end of town I do know it, or rather I did. I used to play Sunday football there in my youth. If memory serves me right, didn't you come to watch a final there not long after we met?'

'Not me, mate, must've been some other girlfriend. You'd hung up your boots by the time we were an item.'

'Are you sure? Wonder who it was then.'

'Just listen to him, Charley, the arrogance of the man. Thinking he played for a team that was good enough to get into a Sunday League final.'

'Cheeky madam. I've probably still got the cups upstairs in the loft, I'll get you to clean them one day.'

Jane laughed. 'In your dreams, chum. How about a whisky and soda? The dishes can wait.'

Pouring the drinks, I noticed some raffle tickets lying on the sideboard. I looked at Jane enquiringly as I handed her drink over.

'Ted wondered if we'd sell some for him.'

'Let me guess. The Policeman's Ball?'

'Don't be facetious. No, it's a community effort to raise money for a sports hall they want to build on wasteland near the park. They've been promised a pound for every one they raise, hence the raffle tickets. I knew you wouldn't mind selling a few and I'll go round the Close. If Ted can't get back to us, we can drop the money off at any police station. Not bad prizes, are they?'

By this time, I was sitting in my armchair, feet up, nursing my drink. 'There'll be no problem getting rid of them. Jeff'll buy some and he'll make sure the rest of the lads stump up for at least one each.' *Shut up, Tom,* I said to myself, *you're waffling again. Just relax and enjoy your drink.*

I'm as sure as I can be that I hadn't been seen at Fromlington Park by anyone who mattered. Apart from the raffle tickets, Ted's visit had been purely social. I'm ashamed for even thinking that Jane could be devious and underhand. She wasn't trying to trap me. I'm the one who was devious and evasive, not her.

I wished again for perhaps the thousandth time that I'd never gone out that fateful night. If I hadn't, none of this would have happened, I'd still be the person I used to be. Not the lying, scheming, prevaricator I'd become, with who knows what mischief lurking below the surface waiting for the right moment to erupt.

'Penny for them?' Toying with her empty glass, Jane watched me with a quizzical expression on her face.

'Sorry, I was miles away. Well not miles actually, I was thinking what a nice change this was. To be warm, well fed and relaxed.'

I wasn't too sure she was convinced but as she didn't say anything further apart from the mildly sarcastic observation. 'Anyone listening to you'd think you'd been doing forced labour in Siberia on starvation rations for months. Instead of which you've been up the road, under cover, for all of four days and with the added benefit of Big Marge's butties.'

Deciding to quit while I was ahead, I changed the subject. 'Anything good on tele tonight?' I asked as I heaved myself out of my chair and went to refill the glasses.

Chapter Eleven

Rush hour traffic, spray, and intermittent drizzle as constant companions on the motorway, didn't cause too much delay the following morning for we arrived at Wilf Oates' office with five minutes to spare.

Climbing the stairs, I wondered whether Wilf'd had a spring clean since my last visit which had been some considerable time ago. But no, Jane's agent still had the scruffiest workplace I've ever come across. Jane says Wilf's office must be bad to have made such an impression on me for she'd always thought I automatically qualified for the title of Britain's Untidiest Man.

Wilf's office had initially been such a shock to me because in my naivete I'd taken it for granted that most people who worked in offices were programmed to be neat, tidy and organised. It was only reluctant office wallahs such as myself, sitting at desks under duress and doing as little paperwork as possible, who had offices as spick and span as the average teenager's bedroom – even down to the obligatory mildewed cups and plates on the floor.

Centre stage in Wilf's office sat (or rather squatted) a huge desk so cluttered I often felt there were things incubating amongst the layers. Things which at the first sign of spring would be ready to burst forth; in what shape or form one could only guess at.

However, in stark contrast to the "Paddy's Market" spectacle of his office, Wilf's mind and appearance were exactly the opposite. The former being razor-sharp, methodical and very organised, while the latter presented a picture of a dapper little man, the epitome of sartorial elegance.

'Hello, you two. Good journey?' Without waiting for a reply, Wilf shook hands with me, gave Jane a kiss on the cheek and cleared two chairs by moving the mile-high stack of papers to another chair, also piled high, where they teetered precariously for a minute or two before deciding to settle down and accept their new home.

'Coffee?' Again, without waiting for an answer, he opened his door and yelled down the corridor in stentorian tones, 'Three coffees with biscuits please, Joan.'

An equally loud reply came back, 'OK, Wilf, five minutes.'

Preliminaries over, Wilf got down to business. Contrary to the muddle of his office he knew exactly where everything was at any given time, as long as some well-meaning busybody hadn't tried to tidy up. He ran a thriving business and had been Jane's agent, in fact her only one, for the past 15 years. He was a popular man, always getting the best deal he could for his authors and illustrators. In return, he expected the best from them. He was especially tough over deadlines.

He quickly scanned Jane's illustrations as we drank our coffee and nibbled biscuits. I should say Jane nibbled and I wolfed, and it was only when she remarked rather pointedly, 'Feeling hungry, Tom?', I noticed the plate was almost empty.

'I seem to be, don't I? We'd better buy another packet when we're shopping.'

'What's with this "we" you ate them all. Anyone'd think you never got fed the way you tucked into them.'

'I must be missing Marge's butties.'

'It'll probably do your waistline good to miss them for one day,' replied Jane smiling sweetly as she nonchalantly leant over and took the last biscuit from under my nose.

'Right,' interrupted Wilf flipping over the last page and closing the folio. 'I gather you've got rather a lot to do today so I won't delay you. But are you free later on?'

We both shook our heads as Jane said, 'We don't have to rush back at any particular time. We've set the whole day aside with the intention of getting everything done in one fell swoop.'

'And we can't go home until we do,' I interjected in a mournful tone.

Wilf laughed. 'You hate shopping that much, Tom! Never mind, we all have to suffer from time to time. How about aiming to get back here by half-five and I'll go through any alterations with Jane; then I'd like to take you both for a meal.' He raised his hand as Jane made to speak. 'I know you aren't dressed for wining and dining, but there's a nice secluded little Italian place just around the corner from here. You'll be able to sit in a dark alcove where no one can see that Wilf Oates is dining with a raven-haired beauty and start rumours.'

Winking at me he continued, 'Good, that's settled then. Tom, why don't you leave your car here, it's easier to get to the city centre by bus than try to find a parking space. It's also cheaper.'

He'd hardly finished before Jane hooted with laughter. 'Tom on a bus! The last time he was on one, the entrance and stairs were at the back and a conductor went along with a quaint old saying like "fares please".'

Smiling at her comments, fervently hoping I wasn't looking guilty I knew there was no way I'd tell Jane that I had been on a bus only recently. This would have meant lying again (the reason why I was on the bus in the first place, and why I hadn't told her earlier). Neither could I agree with her for that would've been another lie. Instead I kept my counsel, which in effect was perhaps just as bad. Lying through the sin of omission.

Standing up, I said, 'That sounds a good idea, Wilf. We'd love to have dinner with you, dressed for it or not, everything accomplished or not.' I turned to Jane. 'Ready, my lovely?'

Helping Jane with her coat, Wilf said, 'The bus stop's right across the road.' He peered at the clock. 'There should be one due in a couple of minutes. Believe it or not, I often take the bus into town these days. Buses and trams, the transport of the future.' He laughed. 'See you later, enjoy your shopping trip, Tom.'

With that parting shot he closed the door behind us, and we could hear him whistling tunelessly as we went down the stairs. I wondered how Joan could stand it and his unkempt, though probably not unique in his trade, way of working. But as she'd been with him since he'd started in business, she must be well used to him and his whistling. Unless of course she was tone deaf.

As with most things, Wilf was right about the bus for one arrived almost right away. Boarding without any sarcastic comments from Jane, I paid our fares, and about 15 minutes later it deposited us and the rest of the travellers in the city centre.

'Where to first' I asked, steering Jane across the busy road. 'And, more to the point, d'you know your way around here?'

'Of course, I do, remember I worked here long enough.'

'Yes. But it's changed so much since then.'

'Only on the surface. Travel agents first, I think, and there it is.' She pointed with her umbrella and was inside the door almost before I'd time to orientate myself.

We had to wait about five minutes before an assistant was free, so we spent the time browsing through brochures for exotic holidays we were never going to take, to places we'd never heard of and at prices that made my eyebrows rise in horror.

'My God,' I whispered to Jane. 'We'd need to be millionaires to afford even a week at this hotel.'

Jane giggled. 'There must be plenty of them around. This one recommends booking early to avoid disappointment.'

'Well we won't have that worry, we couldn't afford a day at these prices, never mind a week.' I took her arm. 'Come on, the assistant's free now.'

It was at least two hours later when we left, but it was time well spent. Every last detail was sorted out, including necessary visas. Jane would leave for New Zealand on the seventeenth of January, in just 10 days' time, and I'd be following three weeks later on the seventh of February. Both flights were from Manchester Airport for connecting flights at Heathrow and then to New Zealand via Singapore. After the wedding and our holiday tour of the island, we'd leave in the middle of May to spend a week in Hong Kong before arriving back in Manchester just before the end of the month.

Feeling very pleased with ourselves and also much lighter in pocket, we paused outside the shop, undecided whether to have a coffee or an early pub lunch. The decision was easy for it was drizzling again and there was a pub a few yards away. Naturally, the pub won.

It was too early for the lunchtime crowds as yet, so we had a choice of seats choosing one by the window; although by the time we'd been served with our hotpots the place was beginning to fill up. We discussed the next step on the agenda, the part I wasn't looking forward to one little bit, namely shopping. Fortunately, Jane knew what she wanted and where to go and patiently explained it all to me amid an increasing hum of background conversation and the clatter of knives, forks, dishes and glasses.

We spent a long time over lunch for we were both very hungry and also had a lot to talk over, not having seen much of each other for over a week – nor were we likely to in the coming week either.

In between mouthfuls of food, Jane jokingly remarked, 'I bet people think we're having an affair.'

I looked at her in astonishment. 'How come?'

'D'you remember when we were courting and used to watch folk in pubs and other places? We were always guessing that the couples sitting side by side not saying a word, were married – and those having animated conversations or holding hands were having an affair. Well, we qualify, for even though we're not holding hands, we are having an animated conversation.'

'Ah yes, I remember now. Also, if I remember rightly, I came up with the theory that they didn't speak because they'd said all there was to say at home. I also hoped that we wouldn't get like that. Are we?'

'Are we what?'

'Like all those silent couples we used to watch when we were young.'

'Not yet, my love, we still find plenty to talk about on the odd occasion you find time to take me out.'

Opening my mouth to protest, Jane forestalled me, 'Only kidding. Shall we get on to discussing our affairs rather than "affairs".'

I let go the thought that she'd been on the verge of commenting how little we'd socialised after my attack, as being unfair to her. It wasn't the sort of thing she'd throw at me, so I polished off my lunch, finished my coffee and ordered drinks before sitting back with a contented sigh. 'OK, where were we before someone interrupted my train of thought with comments about illicit meetings in pubs.'

It was around half past one when we left the pub with Jane looking forward to her shopping spree. On the other hand, I'd have been quite happy to stay put, a very reluctant shopping companion indeed, especially when I saw the crowds.

Jane looked at my face, smiling as she clutched hold of my arm. Obviously not for her benefit, more I think in case I decided to make a break for it. 'Come on, it won't be that bad.'

But it was and much worse. I doggedly stuck at it without too much complaining until just as we were leaving the lingerie department of Debenhams, a voice called, 'Jane, Jane,' stopped us dead in our tracks.

By coincidence or another visit from my old friend fate, the voice belonged to Lois Smart, a children's author, whose latest book Jane had just finished illustrating, so I knew it wasn't going to be a quick 'Hello' and 'Goodbye'.

'Lois, how lovely to see you, what a nice surprise,' said Jane, as the two women hugged and started chatting away nineteen to the dozen.

I coughed to attract their attention. 'Look, I know you two want to have a long natter so I think I'll nip outside for a cigarette. I must say I'm more than ready for one or even ten. How about if I meet you in the coffee shop in say 20 minutes?'

'Poor Tom,' said Lois, 'I gather from that remark you enjoy shopping as much as Bill does.'

'Too true, I'm afraid I'm not one of these so-called New Men who enjoy wandering from counter to counter and shop to shop with their loved ones.'

'Poor old thing,' said Jane laughingly, 'off you go for your smoke.'

So being surplus to their immediate requirements, I took some of the larger shopping bags and entered a lift which had conveniently stopped on its way down; leaving the two women, still talking animatedly, waiting for one to take them to the top floor coffee bar.

Being preoccupied with the shopping bags, endeavouring not to wallop the other occupants as I manoeuvred the awkward packages between my hands, I found myself in the basement, rather than the ground floor when I stepped from the lift. Shrugging my shoulders, I looked around for the stairs, the lift having departed upwards on its merry way by this time.

I made my way towards the exit stairs, my one aim being to get away from the crowds milling around the counters and cash-desks, mostly men I noticed, and then I understood why. It was the hardware department and, as on every other floor, was in the throes of a sale. Pushing my way towards the stairs, the counter on my right caught my attention. It was selling cutlery.

Deliberately stopping, I ran my eyes over the display before doing a complete circle of the counter, studying all that was on offer. Arriving back at my starting point and without hesitation, I quite deliberately selected two needle-thin, finely honed, metal-handled knives. Waiting patiently in the queue at the cash desk, I noticed in an off-hand way that they'd been reduced from five pounds each to three pounds forty-nine.

I was outside smoking my cigarette before the enormity of what I'd done hit me, and I didn't recall lighting up again until the man standing next to me spoke.

'It gets like that doesn't it – shopping. I hate it. This is my third cigarette and I've only been out here a couple of minutes. Oh well back to the fray.' He ground the stub under his foot and disappeared through the swing doors before I'd had time to utter a single word.

Taking several deep breaths, I tried to smoke my cigarette at a less frenetic rate and gradually calmed down. I told myself sternly that I didn't need any knives, especially not finely honed, needle-thin, lethal weapons, such as I'd bought, reduced or otherwise. The best thing I could do would be to drop them in the nearest rubbish bin. Put their purchase down to a rush of blood to the head, sales fever, cold, tiredness or any old wives' tale I cared to drag up.

But I knew I wouldn't. I was going to hang on to those knives come what may and I wouldn't be mentioning them to Jane either. More deceit. I began to wonder if I was developing a split personality caused by the blow to my head. On the one hand, my rational voice was trying to talk sense to the part of me that was intent on vengeance. But that part wasn't listening.

Sighing I looked at my watch. More than 20 minutes had elapsed since leaving Jane, so like the chap before me, I ground my cigarette stub underfoot and prepared to re-enter the store. How many had I smoked! Four judging by the soggy squashed butts around my feet.

This time it wasn't too bad going up in the lift even if I was poked in the ribs and back by what seemed like several umbrella-wielding parcels. Jane and Lois sitting at a table on the far side of the coffee bar had already ordered coffee and scones from a much-harassed waitress, these arrived as I sat down.

Jane smiled 'Good timing there, Tom.'

The two women had apparently finished talking shop, and the conversation went on to weddings, the merits of wearing a hat or otherwise, guest lists – which in our case wouldn't be a problem – and the strange things some people took along to the church.

I liked Lois; she was as I always imagined a children's author would be. She liked her readers, had a marvellous sense of humour and was as mad as a hatter. Looking at her watch, she gave a sudden squawk of alarm. 'My goodness, it's a quarter to five. Must dash. I think I arranged to meet Bill 15 minutes ago but I can't remember exactly where. Never mind it'll come to me on the way.' She hurriedly kissed us, still talking. 'Have a lovely holiday won't you, don't forget to give my love to Sam.'

With that she was gone. A mini-whirlwind, over loquacious and prone to infectious giggling, but in the short time available over coffee she'd succeeded in rousing me from my momentary depression.

'We must go too,' said Jane. 'We haven't got the suitcases yet. I wonder which floor they're on.'

'They're in the basement.'

Jane slipped on her coat as I settled the bill. We then made our way towards the lift, after first gathering up the various bags and packages accompanied by some mild complaints from yours truly. 'I'm sure these have multiplied; I don't remember half of these bags.'

Pressing the lift button, Jane said, 'Don't be daft, you know they haven't. Stop moaning. You've been fed and watered, you should be ready for anything. Now where did you say the luggage was?'

'Ready for anything except more shopping,' I said jovially as we entered the lift, hastily adding 'basement' as Jane stood with her finger hovering over the buttons. The lift made its way down to the floor where I'd made my lethal purchase such a short time ago. I felt totally separated from that episode as if it had happened in another life and to another person.

The basement was much quieter now, the bulk of the shoppers having left, and we took time over our selection without feeling we were in the middle of a stampede. The assistant also had time to advise us and we ended up buying two large cases and one small one thrown in for good measure

There was no question of even attempting to struggle on to a peak-hour bus laden as we were. We were thankful just to relax in the back of a taxi up to Wilf's office.

'My word you've had a good day,' he commented as we dumped everything on his floor, thus adding to the general chaos of the place. 'Cleared out the piggy bank?'

'You could say that,' I replied taking off my mac and dropping on to a chair, surprisingly still empty after our morning visit. 'I might manage to find enough to buy a second-class stamp but that's about it.'

'In that case I'll leave you to contemplate your penury and take Jane off to do her alterations. We'll be half an hour at the most. There's the evening paper if you want it.'

He was right as usual. It seemed no time at all before he was back announcing they'd finished. 'Jane's gone to freshen up, she won't be long. I gather from Jane and those'—he nodded towards our abandoned packages—'it's been a successful day all round. I bet though you're now both tired and hungry.'

'How right you are, Wilf old boy, how right you are, but you forgot the broke bit. In my case, very broke. It'll take years, if ever, to recover from this day's spending spree.'

Wilf gave a loud guffaw. 'Get on with you. You loved every minute of it, and I know you don't begrudge Jane one penny of what you spent.'

Laughing with him, I replied, 'I'd hotly dispute that statement regarding the enjoyment of shopping. It's only ever done under duress. But I agree, Jane is worth every penny she's spent and more.' So saying, I too took myself off to freshen up, feeling more lively after rinsing my hands and face in cold water.

As Wilf had said the restaurant was just around the corner from his office. It had stopped raining, so I threw my raincoat (and its insidious contents) in the boot of my car as we passed. We then went on to enjoy a very welcome meal.

Wilf talked non-stop, or so it appeared to me, and yet he still managed to extract a lot of information about the things we'd bought and our forthcoming trip. Being a much-travelled man, he gave us a few tips on Hong Kong such as where to eat, where to shop (perish the thought I said) and what areas to avoid. He was also a mine of useless but interesting information, most of which was very amusing.

Going back to his office to collect our parcels, we had a last cup of coffee and left Wilf just before nine after promising on pain of death to send at least one postcard. The motorway was quiet, the journey uneventful and we were home in just under an hour.

Leaving Jane to sort through the various shopping bags, I took the dog several times around the block to compensate for his day-long isolation. It was raining again so grabbing my mac from the boot of the car, I removed the two knives from the pocket and slipped them still in their wrappers down the side of the wheel brace. I wasn't actually hiding them, just placing them out of sight of any casual observers – or so I told myself.

By the end of our third circuit it was raining so heavily that Charley went straight up the driveway and sat on the doorstep waiting to be let in. Alone all day or not, he wasn't prepared to get soaking wet in order to alleviate my feelings of guilt.

Worn out, Jane and I didn't even bother to catch the late news on television. Instead we took a hot drink to bed and in no time at all, Jane was fast asleep. I smiled to myself, she and Wilf had consumed rather a lot of wine with their meal, neither having to worry about driving. Kissing her forehead, I turned off the light and heard the town hall clock strike midnight as I settled down and closed my eyes, letting the steady sound of the rain soothe me to sleep.

Chapter Twelve

Tuesday, Wednesday and Thursday came and went in a blur of rivets, screws, wiring, electrical circuits and strong black tea. Jim popped in for a couple of hours each night and his dry wit helped to lift Greg's intense concentration and single-mindedness as his deadline drew ever nearer.

Thursday night, however, around about half past eleven, we hit a snag. Too tired to tackle it there and then we decided to call it a day and face the problem the following morning when our heads would, hopefully, be a bit clearer.

I hadn't visited the cafe at all during the previous four evenings when either Jim or Greg had popped over for the pies. And as there wasn't any change in Jim's manner on his return, I gathered my bête noire hadn't been in residence. Even so, as we were leaving on the Thursday night, there they were, caught in the sweep of my headlights, coming from behind the cafe and making their way towards the alleyway.

Pushing them to the back of my mind I flicked my cigarette through the car window. I wasn't yet ready for them but knew where I'd find them when the time was right. So, negotiating the now familiar potholes, I pointed the car towards home and bed.

On Friday morning when I arrived at the workshop the air was thick with Greg's swearing and cursing; and as he usually only swore to that extent under extreme pressure, I gathered our snag had turned into a minor crisis. I walked in to hear a stream of blasphemies such as I'd not heard since my army days; not even from today's youngsters who tend to string them together instead of using sentences.

'Sorry about the language, Tom,' said Greg looking up as I closed the door. 'But I thought that if I got here early enough, I could sort out the problem and then we'd be able to get stuck in straight away.' He swore some more. 'I've looked at those so-and-so drawings until I'm blue in the face and I've finally come to the conclusion there's a piece of that blasted machine missing.'

Stepping over to the drawing, I looked to where he was pointing then crossed to the machine itself and the pieces still to be fitted. 'I think you're right, Greg, there isn't a piece that shape anywhere, nothing even remotely resembling it. One of our numbered pieces is definitely AWOL; only a small piece I grant you, but essential for all that.'

Greg swore some more before saying, 'I'll make some tea. Thinking time. My first cup since I got here, though I feel the need for something stronger, even if it's only eight in the bloody morning. Still I'll have to settle for tea.'

When he came back with the tea, I was poring over the drawing. 'I should be able to make that piece, Greg. It'll take a good few hours, mind you, but I'm sure between us Jeff and I'll manage it.' Taking the tea, I sipped it gratefully, it really was freezing in that place, although I think Greg's frustration was keeping him warm. He hadn't even switched on his archaic central heating eyesore. Rolling up the drawing, I drained my tea in one gulp, it didn't stay warm for long in that temperature. 'What'll you do in the meantime, stay here?'

'Any idea how long it'll take?'

'Off the top of my head, at least four hours, maybe longer.'

'In that case I think I'll go home and give Kate a shock. Re-introduce myself to her, maybe even have a conversation. I know it's only been two weeks, but it seems an eternity of "Hello" "Goodbye"; the kids think we've split up. I suppose I could do some other work, but I know I won't settle. I feel like the rider in that poem we learnt as kids, where a kingdom was lost for the want of a nail or something as trivial. It had to bloody happen now just when it was going so well.'

'It's known as Murphy's or Sod's Law, Greg. If a job's going too smoothly or ahead of schedule, throw a spanner in the works and watch them flap. Don't worry, we'll do it. I'll give you a ring as soon as it's ready.'

Taking the drawing and leaving Greg to his frustration, I drove to my own workshop, which felt like a sauna after the bleakness of Greg's place, although it was only possibly about five degrees warmer.

I'd spoken to Jeff the previous weekend, explained what was happening at Greg's and then given him our news. He'd assured me there'd be no problem regarding the workshop, but I'd stressed that I'd discuss things thoroughly once Greg's machine was up and running.

Jeff was therefore surprised to see me, looking up from his work as I entered the small canteen situated just off my office. His work at that moment consisted of berating the youngest member of the workforce, Mike who was all of 19, on the merits of making a proper brew. Jeff never raised his voice, but his brand of dour Scots sarcasm was guaranteed to turn any newcomer to a quivering jelly. As Mike had been with us for three years, he was well used to him and didn't turn a hair; just fished out another cup for me.

When Jeff and I were in the office, I explained the problem and after studying the drawing, he came to the same conclusion as myself, which was that a piece could be made, but it'd take the best part of the morning. 'It's a peculiar shape is it not, Tom? Will you be wanting to work on it yourself?'

I shook my head 'No, Jeff. Unless you're in the middle of something else, you go ahead and get started. I'll catch up on some work here.'

'There's nothing that canna wait awhile.' As he left the office, I heard him call to Mike to get his finger out as they had work to do.

It was warm enough for me to take off my coat and settling in my chair, I surveyed my desk. It had been well over two weeks since I'd been in the office and while Jeff had seen to everyday matters, there were things that really needed sorting out. What better time than now. The Christmas cards and decorations had been removed but the old calendars still adorned the walls and desk.

Hanging a new calendar on the wall, I took the rest, mostly girly ones, out to the canteen for the lads to share amongst themselves. I then spent some time clearing the paperwork from the top of the desk. Most of which was consigned straight to the rubbish bin. I didn't bother Jeff; he was quite capable of getting on with the job without any interference from me. My turn would come later when I'd be fitting the capacitor and essential leads to the completed piece.

I pulled open my desk drawer with the intention of carrying out my annual clear-out. I've a habit of throwing telephone messages and scribbled notes into the capacious drawers and getting rid of them about once a year. I do have a part-time secretary and general 'do-it-all' whom I share with Arthur Stanhope a painter and decorator across the way. An arrangement which has worked very well for all concerned for a number of years.

This particular drawer of mine, however, is known as the 'bottomless pit' a voluntary no-go area to all and sundry except me. Meg Ferguson, my typist, refers to it as the 'Bermuda Triangle of Brimstage' arguing that once anything gets in there, that's the last time it's seen in this life. To a degree she's right. It's amazing how much rubbish gets shoved in there during the year, and here was an early opportunity to clear out the accumulation of detritus and debris. Thus, I spent the next half hour reducing one pile of rubbish while building another in the wastepaper basket.

It was as I neared the bottom of the drawer that I came across my hospital appointment card. I looked at the dates – ten months since the attack and six months since my last appointment. It all seemed a lifetime away and yet I can recall each sickening impact of the attack as if it were yesterday; can still feel my face hitting that pavement. The visible scars may have faded, apart from a crooked nose, but the invisible ones were only just below the surface, and they went very deep.

I still suffered recurring nightmares and broken sleep. Jane knew about my inability to sleep properly unless I took a sleeping pill or had a couple of whiskies, but I'd never told her about the nightmares. I don't know whether she guessed or not; if she did, she never mentioned it. The whole episode had shaken her and Sam very badly. In fact, Sam was all for cancelling her exchange and rushing home at once. Jane's confidence had also taken a knock since the attack and undermined her faith in the basic goodness of humanity.

Thus, the ripples had spread, touching both friends and relatives alike. In the intervening months I was often reminded of John Donne's words about no man being an island. I may have been the recipient of the beating, but the whole incident had made victims of other innocents apart from myself.

We had, on the other hand, met many kind and caring people from the staff at the hospital through to the police officer, Ted Jarvis, who became a friend, plus of course friends and neighbours. Even our paperboy had sent me a get-well card. Now if Sam had cut short her visit to New Zealand, she might not now be getting married – so perhaps everything is pre-ordained. Maybe so, but did it have to be so painful and humiliating!

I contemplated why it was I wasn't so jittery these days about being out on my own late at night. It might have been down to sheer tiredness and the long hours I was working which took my mind off the terrors of the night, or again it might be because I could now identify my assailants. They were no longer simply beings of my nightmares. They had become flesh and blood. I had seen their faces. I knew their names. I pondered about the pair a while longer before tearing the card into shreds and tossing the pieces into the basket. That card represented a shadowy Tom Marshall. Not the man I was before the attack and certainly not the Tom Marshall

SOFTLY TO THE QUAY

who only yesterday had calmly bought two deadly weapons and had just as calmly had hidden them away.

Unaware I was staring into space (this was getting to be a habit) I visibly jumped when a voice said, 'Penny for them, Tom?'

Gathering my wits, I looked up to see Arthur Stanhope standing in the doorway a puzzled look on his face. 'Morning, Arthur. I'm supposed to be clearing last year's stockpile of rubbish from these drawers, ready for the next lot. I've been here I don't know how long, and only cleared one. Mind you it was the worst of the lot. What can I do for you?'

'Meg's eldest phoned. She's got the flu and won't be in for at least another week. I said I'd let you know, save another phone call. How's tricks, you got much on? My Christmas and New Year rush is over, thank God and things are pretty quiet at the moment. Any bits of typing I've got can wait.'

'No panic here either. The lads are working on some long-term stuff and I'm helping Greg Mathieson. You remember him, don't you? Now there is a panic. I wouldn't be here now if a piece of the infernal machine he's putting together wasn't missing. That's what Jeff's doing at the moment – creating the missing link.'

'I'll be off then,' said Arthur. 'Never let it be said that I interrupted a man when he's spring cleaning, although I could've sworn you were just staring into thin air. Are you practising telekinesis these days?'

With that parting shot and a wave of his hand, he was gone. Quickly clearing the rest of the rubbish from the desk, I left some stuff for Meg on her return, made an appointment with the bank for Jeff and myself and then called Jane.

'Ah, my psychic husband. I was just thinking about you but didn't want to interrupt you.'

'I'm not phoning from Greg's, I'm at the office, there's a problem with "Flora".

'Go on I'll buy it, who's Flora?'

'That's what young Jim's taken to calling the machine.'
I explained about the missing piece. 'Did you want me for
something specific. There's nothing wrong is there?'

'No. I just wanted to tell you that Sam's letter has finally
arrived – reams of it.'

'Hang on a tick, love, I'll see how Jeff's getting on. If there's
still some way to go, I'll pop home for a sandwich.'

Laying the phone down, I went into the workshop where
Jeff so engrossed in what he was doing was totally unaware of
me until I tapped him on the shoulder.

'It's coming along nicely, Tom,' he replied in answer to my
query. 'I reckon another hour should do it.'

'Good. It's coming up to half-eleven now. I'm nipping home
for a bite to eat. If Greg rings in the meantime, that's where I'll
be. I'll be back around half-twelve. See you later.' Back in the
office I picked up the phone. 'Jane, I'm leaving now. You can
start making the tea.'

After a hasty sandwich, at least three cups of tea, the pleasure of eating and drinking in warmth and comfort and
wading through Sam's letter, I headed back to my workshop.
Jeff had completed his piece of the jigsaw and looking at the
size of it, I was amazed at how such a minute piece of metal
could cause so much disruption. But then as Greg had said,
"all for the want of a nail." It did, however, take me the best
part of another hour to complete the necessary wiring.

Phoning Greg to give him the good news, I said, 'You can
stop pacing the floor and biting your nails, it's done. I'll see
you back at the Quays at two o'clock.'

His sigh of relief was palpable even to Jeff standing a few
feet away. But the four hours had stretched to six on this the
last Friday of Greg's schedule, leaving only two and a half
days before he was due to start production.

'Bye, folks,' I said gathering up the precious piece of metal
and preparing to leave. 'Thanks a lot, see you all on Monday,
I hope.'

Greg got to the Quay before me and turning my car around to face away from the water, I drew up alongside his and went to join him. I carried the missing link as though it was gold dust and the fervent hope it would fit without too much blood, sweat and tears.

Our luck was in. The new piece needed only a few minor adjustments before it finally fitted snugly into position and the appropriate connections made.

We then made good time for the rest of the day and early evening. And as everything was going smoothly, we didn't even stop for a bite to eat or any of our several cups of tea until a plaintive voice was heard coming from the back of the machine.

'I don't know about you two, but if I don't get something to eat very soon, I'm going to expire here and now and will probably become merged with this contraption. Then if anyone ever asks after me, you'll be able to say, "Oh, young Jim! That's part of him over there. That's his open mouth where we pour the resin. Oh, didn't you know? He died of starvation, poor lad. He's now at one with Flora."'

Greg and I looked at each other, peered round the back of the machine at Jim, simultaneously looked at the clock, which read a quarter past nine, and both burst out laughing.

'Doesn't time fly when you're having fun,' said Greg. 'OK, Jim, I can take a hint as well as the next man. I'll just finish off this bit here and then pop over to Freddie's.

'I'll go.' I got to my feet. 'Two pies each?'

'Three for me,' called Jim. 'And I don't care who goes as long as it's soon. Very, very soon. I'm not sure I'll have the strength to get up off the floor, and I'm positive I'll be shaking far too much to be of use filling the kettle. It must be all of four hours since the last morsel of food or the last drop of liquid passed these pale lips of mine. If I were a Victorian maiden, I'd have fainted clean away by now.'

'If you were a Victorian maiden, you wouldn't be stretched out on an engineering workshop floor down by the docks, late on a Friday evening pining for a pie and a mug of tea, that I can tell you. Unless of course you were up to no good,' said Greg. 'Come on, shift your emaciated body and get that bloody kettle on.'

'And that's another thing. Tea.' Jim was still having his say as he emerged on all fours from behind the machine. 'My grandad said I'd be drinking tea all day long when I told him where I'd be working. Can't say I've seen much evidence of that today. Come to think of it, I didn't even like tea before I came here. Now Grandad says I make it as if I've been taught by a Cocky Watchman on a building site, whatever that means.'

Still smiling at Jim's words, I walked across to the cafe, pushed open the door and entered the smoky atmosphere. Freddie said the pies would take about five minutes so turning lightly from my stance at the counter, I surreptitiously surveyed the corner near the door. My lighthearted thoughts quickly evaporated as I espied them talking to the usual third party. I tried to deduce whether they were right or left-handed from the way cigarettes were held, cups lifted, and things passed, and concluded they were both right-handed.

Turning back to the counter, hopefully before anyone became aware I was watching, I paid for the pies and left the cafe wondering why I was so concerned whether Billy and Bobby were right or left-handed. Once more the thought crossed my mind that I was two people in one body. One did read of such cases. On the one hand an ultra-egotist planning with cool precision the ultimate crime; while my other self was quiet, reserved and so very frightened. Once again, I found myself wishing for the thousandth time that I'd stayed home on that fateful night.

Chapter Thirteen

'I knew you'd forget!'

'Of course, I haven't forgotten,' I said with false confidence.

'Oh yes you have. Otherwise, you wouldn't be lying stretched out on the couch ready for a lazy evening of either sleeping or watching television, whichever comes first.' Laughing, she prodded my middle. 'Come on, admit it. You haven't a clue.'

'Alright, I give in. I have forgotten, though it can't be too disastrous such as our anniversary, or Great Aunt Agnes's hundredth and tenth birthday. Or even the day nearest to the first Sunday of the last Friday when we moved in here, because, my beloved, you are smiling.'

'And you're talking a load of rubbish as usual.' Sitting on the arm of the couch, Jane continued. 'Seriously I don't mind if you don't want to come; after all, you didn't know whether you would've finished at Greg's anyway.'

Realisation dawned. 'The Poetry Awards?' Jane nodded.

As well as being an accomplished illustrator, Jane also, as she puts it, dabbled in poetry and was one of the founder members and judges of the local annual poetry competition. This competition, open to residents within a 20-mile radius of our town hall, had been running for about 10 years now and was proving more popular every year.

Today, or rather this evening, was the big event for the 12 finalists who would be reading their poems in public for the first time; the winner receiving a cup and a modest cheque. Due to the increasing popularity of the event, the venue for this year's awards had been moved from our local church hall to the much larger premises of the village hall at Asherton about 10 miles away. Myself, plus other assorted husbands, wives and partners, usually went along as the general help. Setting out chairs, organising refreshments and whatever else was required in the way of brawn rather than brain.

But Jane was right. Not really expecting Greg's "Flora" to be ready with time to spare, I'd completely forgotten about the competition and was indeed ready to settle down for a relaxing night in front of the television. Swinging my feet to the floor without so much as a sigh, I stood up and stretched. 'No, I want to come. How much time do I have?'

'I'd like to leave in about half an hour. Say 20 minutes to get there, which should leave another 20 or so to get the chairs and whatnot organised. Bill and Primrose—'

I interrupted with a snort of derision. 'Primrose! Primrose! Anyone less like a delicate flower I've yet to meet.'

'Now Tom stop it. She can't help her name. You know she's a very nice woman underneath all that blubber.'

'You're right, I shouldn't be so rude. I am very fond of her, it's just that the name and the initial reality don't go together whatsoever. But after a while, she's just Primrose who shifts the tables while the men make the tea.'

'Now you are exaggerating,' said Jane laughing. 'Where was I before you interrupted? Bill and Primrose will be there around seven o'clock and the others should arrive shortly after; that's if Timothy doesn't get lost.'

I headed for the door. 'Timmy get lost! Never.' And made a quick exit before Jane could reply.

I thought about the judges as I washed and changed. A mixed bunch of diverse characters with one thing in common – a love of poetry. I admit to being a complete Philistine when it comes to matters of pentameters, iambics and bigfoot spondees, but I enjoy listening to the readings at these shindigs. Bill and I usually did a little judging of our own, mine usually on the back of a cigarette packet, and I've never managed to tally with the judges' selection, not even Jane's. One day, I promised myself, I'll get it spot on.

Arriving at the hall sometime later and parking as near to the entrance as possible, we entered through the great double doors into what appeared to me to be a vast cavern of a place. Fortunately, someone had had the foresight to switch the heating on, so it was quite warm. We helpers got stuck in right away, arranging chairs, setting up the microphone and the judges' table and sorting out the refreshments.

There were eight of us in all, helping through either coercion or a genuine interest in the proceedings. I worked in tandem with Bill, Primrose's husband, as slight as she was big. Jack Spratt and his wife came to mind. We were usually quite quick and efficient, but we'd hardly got the first dozen rows of chairs sorted out before people were pouring through the doors. There had been several already waiting when Jane and I arrived.

Setting the last two chairs in place at the back of the room, Bill and I sat down both feeling hot and sweaty and glad of the rest. The hall was extremely well heated, in stark contrast to the walk-in freezer of a place that was Greg's workshop.

'Half an hour isn't long enough for this hall,' sighed Bill wiping the perspiration from his forehead. 'It was enough for St Peter's but this place is twice the size. Mind you the way this competition keeps growing, we're likely to end up at the Albert Hall before long.'

'At least we won't have to arrange the seats there,' I muttered as Timothy walked onto the stage and a hush fell over the audience, broken only by the sound of the doors closing with a resounding crack.

'Let battle commence,' said Bill from the side of his mouth. 'At least Tim made it on time – I wonder how early he set out.'

'Some time yesterday, I shouldn't wonder. He really—' I got no further because the woman in front turned round and glared with such ferocity, we both felt like naughty boys caught smoking behind the bike shed.

Timothy cleared his throat. 'Good evening, ladies and gentlemen, welcome to the new venue for this year's poetry finals. For those of you who've attended our little gatherings in the past, you'll be familiar with the procedure; and for those of you who haven't, well, the programme explains all. As per usual, the finalists are listed in alphabetical order. We therefore commence the proceedings with our first finalist – Miss Mary Chalmers.'

The first six went through their readings with Bill and I comparing notes and points, so I wasn't looking at the stage when Tim announced the next entrant. Arnold Perry. The name meant nothing to me. Just an ordinary run-of-the-mill name. However, when Mr Arnold Perry started reading, I sat up with a jerk, my eyes riveted on the nondescript, ordinary looking little man with the plain ordinary name, standing at the front of the stage.

That voice. Neither ordinary nor nondescript but one which elicited a familiar ice-cold feeling on the back of my neck despite the heat in the hall. That voice. It had to be the man from the cafe. The chill on the nape of my neck confirmed it. His reading was apparently excellent judging by the prolonged applause he received, though for the life of me I hadn't heard one single word. I only listened to the voice, not what he said.

But as the applause died down, I had a moment of doubt, such as I'd had when I'd first seen Billy in town. Was I mistaken? The two didn't really go together – nefarious goings-on in a dockside cafe and the writing of poetry. Nevertheless, history is full of such anomalies. Take Nero for one or Hitler, who was reputed to have been something of an artist. I was so stunned, or to put it in the vernacular, gobsmacked, that I didn't remember a single thing about the last five finalists, neither readers nor poems. I must have been on automatic pilot though, for I was still comparing marks with Bill.

During the interval I didn't have much time to dwell on this unexpected side of villainy, being kept busy in the kitchen, washing and drying an endless mountain of crockery. But there was one moment of panic when I was having my own coffee at the back of the refreshment room. The wild thought crossed my mind that if the little man was here, were the other two also lurking about? I looked around frantically before common sense asserted itself. There was no earthly reason why he should mix his business and private lives. Apart from that, I wasn't even sure the two "B's" could read, much less have an interest in poetry. I didn't know if the little man spotted me amongst the crowd and if so whether he'd remember me from the cafe. Why should he and what did it matter? My quarrel wasn't with him.

The judges had their refreshments in a separate room while they made their decisions and so, after everyone was more or less back in their seats, Tim strode on stage to announce the results. Bill and I ruminated on our choices compared to the judges, and as usual, we didn't have any of the runners-up listed, although Bill did have the winner down as a possible third or fourth.

The winner, as fate would have it, was Arnold Perry. But as I'd not listened to one single word of his initial reading, I was in no position to comment, not that my judgement was anything to go by. He went on stage to receive his trophy and cheque and to read his winning entry once more. This time I gave my whole attention to Mr Arnold Perry, as he began reading "Journey to the Sea".

Snow-capped mountains cold and bleak,
Way too high for goats and sheep.
Await the spring.

It was quite a long poem, ending with the lines –

In a myriad of channels, the waters hide.
Then all do vanish to an incoming tide.

After his reading and the ensuing applause, Perry gave a stiff little bow, made a very hesitant speech of thanks (was this the same authoritative man from the cafe?) and left the stage.

His exit signalled the end of the evening apart from a final word from Tim wherein he expressed the hope that everyone had enjoyed the evening, concluding with a big thank you to all who had helped. As people were taking their leave, I espied Jane, talking to Arnold Perry, look around as if searching for someone.

I made a hasty exit into the kitchen just in case it was me she was looking for and began helping Primrose with the last of the washing up. Whether Jane had been looking for me or not, I wasn't taking any chances. I had no desire whatsoever to be introduced to Mr Arnold Perry in either of his guises – prize-winning poet or small-time criminal.

When I returned to the hall almost everyone had gone, including Arnold Perry, so Bill and I reversed the process of the early part of the evening by gathering the chairs and stacking them at the back of the room. Once we'd made sure that everywhere was clean and tidy, we helpers were at last able to take our own leave. Tim had been one of the first to go, though the general consensus was that he'd definitely be the last to arrive home, having forgotten the way.

In the car, Jane gave a sigh of contentment as she fastened her seatbelt. 'I think I can safely say that the evening was a success.'

'It was certainly a good turnout. I wouldn't have thought there were so many aficionados of poetry about; there were far too many people there to be the friends and relatives of all the finalists.'

'Poetry, my dear Tom, is alive and well and thriving up and down the country. We had a difficult choice over the winner though, Arnold Perry won by the narrowest of margins. He seems to be a nice chap but one of those people whose voice doesn't match their appearance. Like a voice you hear on the phone and imagine someone like Sean Connery and get Cleggy from *Last of the Summer Wine* instead.'

I was trying to come to terms with Arnold Perry as Sean Connery when Jane said, 'I had a chat with him afterwards and he told me he's been writing poetry since he was a schoolboy but has only been entering competitions for the last year or so. He was tickled pink that he'd won this one. His mother was with him, but they had to rush off; he said he doesn't like her to be out too late on these damp winter nights. She suffers with bronchitis or something chesty. He came across as a very caring and considerate sort of person but'—she snuggled further down into her seat—'I still can't equate the voice with the reality. He'd make a wonderful radio announcer.'

Appearances are very deceptive, I thought but didn't dare voice my opinions to Jane. Everyone has to have had a mother and obviously Arnold Perry cared for his. He too had two sides to his nature. Another part of me wondered if he'd rushed off because he had to attend to his night-time affairs. I mused on this and the shock of seeing him in a totally unexpected environment. Another coincidence in the chain of coincidences that were continually cropping up regarding the two "B's" et al. But as usual I failed to find a satisfactory answer to my musings.

Chapter Fourteen

On the day of Jane's departure, we were up with the proverbial lark. But if there were any birds around in any shape or form, they were apparently using their common sense, keeping their heads down and having a lie-in. There were no birds singing their little hearts out in our neck of the woods that's for sure.

The reason we were up so early was that according to Jane there were still a million and one things that just had to be done, even though her flight wasn't due to leave until three in the afternoon. To be fair, she had planned to do most, if not all, the million and one things the previous evening but Greg had arranged a small dinner party at a local restaurant, which put paid to that little scheme.

Along with Jane and myself, Greg and his wife Kate, Jim had brought along his grandfather. The meal was by way of a thank you from Greg for all our hard work and our wives' tolerance. What Bert (Jim's grandfather) thought about being classed as a wife he didn't say. An enormous weight had been lifted from Greg's shoulders with the completion of the machine, visible in his step, his manner and most of all in his appalling jokes.

The last screw was finally turned, and the last nut finally tightened around about half past ten on the Saturday night when Jim was given the signal honour of switching on the machine. Not that he considered it an honour of course. His exact words were, 'You're only asking me to do it in case me and "Flora" both light up like Blackpool Lights.'

His fears, however, were groundless and after some initial teething troubles when the tubs were coming out all shapes and sizes, "Flora" was now working to full capacity and Greg considered he was on schedule for his deadline; hence he felt he could now relax. As well as wining and dining us in style, he also presented the ladies with miniature margarine tubs containing pearl earrings.

As he presented Kate and Jane with their tubs, he remarked to Jim and myself, 'I didn't bother getting you two any as I noticed your ears weren't pierced.'

'We can always remedy that,' said Jim and I in unison and Bert commented that he'd had his done when he was in the Merchant Navy.

He concluded with, 'The holes have closed up now, of course, but I'm sure I could locate them if there's a couple of pearls in the offing.'

The evening continued in much the same vein, and it was quite late when we eventually left the restaurant amid good-byes and promises of postcards.

Jane was rather quiet in the taxi on the way home, and I put it down to the lateness of the hour, plus all the things she thought she still had to do the following day. But when I returned with a reluctant dog (as it was neither wet nor freezing, he was ready for a longer sojourn), Jane had poured us both a nightcap, idly nursing hers as she stared into the fire.

Sitting on the couch, I put my arm across her shoulders. 'What's the matter, sweetheart? Worried about flying all that way on your own?'

'Don't be ridiculous, Tom, you know I'm not.' She snuggled down into the crook of my arm. 'But I am concerned about you. This is the first time we'll have been separated since your attack. I know it still bothers you because it affects your sleep. As a matter of fact, in the last three weeks you've been having nightmares again. And I know it's the same nightmare because you always call out the same thing. "skippity hop, skippity hop" as if you were chanting a children's rhyme. I have to hold you tight for a few minutes before you calm down. What's happened, Tom, to reopen the wounds? What are you keeping from me? I can't go away not knowing. Granted it's pretty late in the day, but there hasn't been much chance to discuss things before now.'

Stunned, I was silent for a moment sipping my drink to give me time to think. Then I said, 'I didn't tell you about my nightmares because in my naivete I thought you weren't aware of them.' *Stupid, stupid Tom*, I chided myself. *How could Jane not know if she was comforting you?* But then I'd not been aware of that comfort nor that I'd spoken aloud. I only knew the nightmares had come back. 'Also, I didn't want you getting upset and spoil the enjoyment of your plans by reopening old wounds. As to why the nightmares have returned, I can only put it down to the excessively long hours and concentration I've been putting in lately. My normal sleep patterns disrupted or something like that.'

That spiel sounded lame even to my ears, and I hated myself for lying once again to Jane. It wasn't usually part of my nature to lie to anyone, especially my wife. But I couldn't tell her the real reason for the return of my nightmares. How I'd discovered the identities of my attackers, knew where they hung out and had, in fact, been round the home of one of them.

She might just understand my obsession. Compulsion! But wouldn't necessarily agree or approve. I couldn't tell her at this late stage. There was no way I could let her go off to see our daughter with that on her mind. The decision wouldn't be mine anyway it would be hers. And knowing Jane, she'd immediately cancel her plans and wait until we could both go together. In the meantime, she'd stick to me like glue.

I stroked her hair hoping my inner turmoil wasn't showing in my voice, that I sounded as I usually did after a good meal and several drinks – although by now I was stone cold sober and desperate not to upset her.

'You can't change your plans at this late stage, love. You know how much you've been looking forward to having Sam all to yourself for a few weeks. Imagine how disappointed she'll be if you're not there to go shopping with her, she's been hanging on for that very reason. Anyway, think of all the nattering you've got to catch up on. It'd be a shame if you miss the opportunity. How often in the future will you be able to have her all to yourself? I'll be alright, after all, it's only for three weeks and there are enough people around should I need anyone. But I won't, I know I won't. As I said I put the nightmares down to the worry of the job but now that Flora's up and running, they'll disappear.'

Putting my glass down, I stood, pulling Jane to her feet. 'Come on, it's late, time we were in bed, especially if we've got to be up early. You with your million and one things.' She laughed as I continued with a groan, 'And I've got to be at the dentist's at a quarter past eight. What a horrible thought to wake up with; I might just cancel...'

'Oh no you don't, Tom Marshall. You know you won't make another appointment if you do; you'll just keep putting it off and putting it off – I know you and dentists only too well. Leave things as they are, just another early morning for you.'

'The only thing to be said for going that early is it's nice not to have the thought of a visit to the dentist hanging over me all day.' By this time, I'd taken the empty glasses into the kitchen, turned off the fire and was making my way upstairs followed by Jane. I was congratulating myself on a neat change of conversation when she spoke again.

'You're very good, Tom, at diverting subjects away from things you don't want to discuss. But if I thought for one minute you were keeping something from me, I wouldn't hesitate about cancelling my plans, late in the day or not. As it is, I'll take your word for it, although I'm not entirely convinced.'

As Jane went into the bathroom, I was glad she couldn't see my face, she'd have known right away I was lying. I felt a heel but knew there was just no way on earth I was ever going to tell her the truth. Strangely enough (also fortunately) I didn't have any nightmares, not even about dentists and as far as I was aware spent a peaceful, dreamless night.

So here I was reluctantly driving through the sleet and rain which had greeted me as I left the house. Perfect. Just bloody perfect. What more could a man ask? The dentist and grotty weather to boot. The situation wasn't improved when I arrived only to be told that Mr Murdoch was going to be late

'He's had a puncture,' said the receptionist. 'It might be another half an hour before he gets here. Do you want to wait, or make another appointment?'

It was very tempting to cut and run but Jane was right. If I didn't stay until he arrived, I knew I wouldn't be back this side of Christmas. 'No, I'm here now I might as well hang on.'

Sitting in the warm waiting room idly flicking through the usual magazines, I settled for an old *Reader's Digest* which looked as though it had been around for some considerable time. When I checked the date, I saw that it was all of three years old. Nevertheless, I read a couple of articles, enjoyed the jokes and asides printed at the bottom of the pages, smiling to myself as I turned over a page and came across an article entitled "Delinquency. Who to Blame – Family or Society". There were several arguments by various learned American psychologists, two of which were not so couched in gobbledegook they actually made sense. Their argument was that delinquency was due either to an over-indulged childhood, or severe deprivation or rejection during the same period of growth, with the overall consensus favouring the first theory.

The article pointed out that delinquents (I wondered if that word was still part of psychologists' jargon, after all it had been written more than three years ago) in the first category had every whim gratified as a child and every action condoned. "They were favoured and forgiven in everything, which in turn led to selfish and demanding behaviour plus a very low tolerance for frustration. They had difficulty in adjusting to authority, difficulty in tolerating monotony and routine and also suffered from a lack of discipline and impoliteness." (unquote) The article concluded that such people "whose lives are one continuous search for gratification are miserable when not indulged and bored when they are indulged." (unquote)

However, before I had time to fully absorb these theories or to wonder if they applied to my pet protagonists the receptionist popped her head around the door of the, now not so empty, waiting room. 'Mr Murdoch's finally arrived, if you'd like to come through, Mr Marshall. He won't be long.'

Twenty minutes later I was once more nosing my way slowly through the traffic; my teeth feeling clean and shiny, which was more than could be said for the weather. It was much worse than when I'd set out, and I needed all my wits to negotiate both vehicles and pedestrians, large and small and all with the same purpose in mind. And that purpose was to get to their destination as quickly as possible, out of that foul weather.

The concentration needed to get home safely took care of any ideas regarding the opinions in the *Reader's Digest*. They were relegated to the back burner of my mind, to simmer slowly until I was ready to assimilate them at a more convenient time.

Chapter Fifteen

Jane was still in her dressing gown when I got home, busy trying to cram parcels of various shapes and sizes into an already overburdened suitcase.

Indicating a further pile of packages – wedding presents dropped off by friends and relatives – she said with a grimace as she sat on her case, 'I'm going to have to leave those for you to bring for as well as being overweight, the case, not me, it's likely to burst at the seams before I've even left the house. How'd you get on? You've been gone so long I thought you must be having problems. But then I'd have heard the screams from here if you were having a tooth out or, horror of horrors, the dreaded drill.'

'Ha, very funny. My teeth are perfect as it happens. Mr Murdoch was the problem. He'd had a puncture so was late and then I had to practically crawl home. The weather's terrible. It won't be a pleasant journey to the airport if that sleet doesn't ease up.' I sighed and pointed to the suitcase. 'You'll have to take some more stuff out to make it anything like manageable. Have you packed for the duration? I'll get on with breakfast and leave you to tackle this lot again.'

'That sounds good. I'm starving, I've been fighting with this case since you left the house, in between answering the phone. It's hardly stopped.' It was her turn to sigh as she contemplated the bulging case and the parcel and clothes-strewn bedroom. 'Oh well, back to the struggle.'

I left the bedroom as Jane started unpacking the top layers, throwing them into my empty suitcase before going back to rearranging her own, in a last-ditch attempt to comply with

SOFTLY TO THE QUAY

both the weight allowance and the breaking strain of locks and straps.

It wasn't long before eggs were frying, bacon and sausages sizzling and the toast burning. Fortunately, the dog's rather fond of buttered charcoal.

'It's ready,' I called up the stairs. 'Come on before I wolf the lot, I'm starving.'

'I don't know about packing for the duration, but this looks as if you intend stoking up for the whole time you'll be on your own. Or is there something you haven't told me? Are we expecting the five thousand for breakfast?' Nibbling on a piece of bacon, Jane looked at the laden plates.

'I got a bit carried away. Never mind I'm sure we'll shift most of it, we need to be well fuelled to face that motorway in this weather. Anyway, what we don't eat no doubt Charley'll finish.' The dog wagged his tail in agreement. I swear he can lipread.

Taking our time, we talked as we ate, mainly about the weather and the numerous things Jane had listed for me to do, or not, as the case may be. This list was growing ever longer as other things sprang to my wife's mind, and it was getting to the stage where there were nearly enough pages to paper the bathroom.

We talked about Charley and how my brother-in-law spoils him rotten. At the mention of John's name, the dog's ears pricked up and he looked expectantly towards the door.

'No worries on that front,' laughed Jane.

We were on our second pot of tea when the phone calls started; at least we'd managed to eat our breakfast in peace. It was as if the world and his wife, not to mention their sisters, brothers, aunts and uncles to boot, were ringing to wish Jane a safe journey and to send best wishes to Sam and Tim. After about the tenth call, the dog shook himself and stalked off to his basket in a huff, putting one paw over his eyes before burying his head. Whether it was the constant ringing of the phone or the unusual activity taking place in the house, but he was most put out that his usually peaceful Thursday morning was being disrupted.

We left for the airport around noon to allow plenty of time for the journey. A journey which normally would take about 45 minutes but could take twice as long on a day such as this. The Weather God, however, decided to be kind and took pity on us for conditions improved slightly and the sleet and rain eased a little, but the spray thrown up by the other traffic on the motorway still made the journey hazardous. All in all, the trip took half an hour longer than usual, and it was with relief that I pulled into the airport car park.

It had been a quiet journey, neither of us had spoken much. I'd been too busy concentrating on getting there in one piece for chit-chat, idle or otherwise, although it was unusual for Jane to be quiet for such a long period. But she waited until she'd checked in and got rid of her luggage, fortunately only slightly overweight, before voicing her concerns. 'I'm still worried, you know, Tom.' It was as if now when the practicalities had been taken care of, she could focus her mind on the emotional aspects which were bothering her.

We were sitting by the window enjoying a very welcome cup of coffee, idly watching the planes, which appeared impervious to the weather. I took hold of Jane's hand. 'Love, I'm a big boy. I have been left at home alone before now. Please stop worrying or as you're so fond of saying, we're going to end up with me worrying about you worrying about me which won't help either of us.'

Jane smiled. 'I know. Normally it wouldn't bother me, but I've still got this sneaking suspicion you're keeping something from me.'

Cursing the intuitiveness of women and my wife's in particular, I kept my face and voice as bland as possible, as I again lied in my teeth. I don't know about being given a clean bill of health it's a wonder they hadn't rotted in my mouth with all the lying I'd done lately. 'Jane, sweetheart, I'm not keeping anything from you. I'll be on my own for what three weeks. Twenty-one days. Most of those will be spent at work plus all the other bits and pieces you've lined up for me. I won't starve. I won't forget to water the plants, cancel the milk, take Charley to Grace and John's, leave the spare keys with them and the Ashburtons. Clean the house before I leave, turn off the central heating and hot water, make sure all the windows and doors are locked and get myself to the airport and on to the plane on Thursday the eleventh of February at 10pm. Oh yes, I almost forgot. Cancel the papers and put out the rubbish.' Pausing, I took a deep breath. 'Now, I don't think that leaves much time for brooding, moping or getting into mischief. Do you?'

Jane started laughing, which had been my intention. 'I'm sorry, Tom, you're right. I'll try to put you completely out of my mind for the next three weeks.'

'Don't you dare. Just think of me occasionally and ring now and then, which is precisely what I'll be doing.'

About to say something else, she was interrupted by a tannoy announcement. 'Will all passengers travelling on Air New Zealand, Flight AN One Three, please assemble at Gate 24.'

'That's me, come on.' Finishing our coffee, we gathered her bits and pieces and joined the general melee towards Gate 24. Stopping just short of the entrance, Jane dropped her bags and threw her arms around me, clinging tightly as if this was our last farewell and she was never going to see me again. 'I love you so much, Tom. Please take care.' Giving me a last kiss, she was gone before I could say a word, which would have been difficult anyway, due to the huge lump sticking in my throat.

Along with many others, I waited with mixed emotions until the plane took off, watching it taxi ponderously down the runway before lifting its enormous bulk off the ground and flying off into the late wintry afternoon.

Recovering my car, I joined the queue to leave the airport, joining another to get on to the motorway. Once in the stream of traffic, I made good time in spite of the spray and arrived home just before five. I was tired, drained and full of conflicting feelings. The house already felt empty. But I was also glad Jane wasn't here. For now, I could single-mindedly pursue my half-formed idea.

I made a cup of tea, fed the dog and took him for a short walk, short by mutual consent for it was turning into a bitterly cold evening. Later I cooked myself some steak and chips which I ate in front of the television. The news was as gloomy as the weather. Finishing my makeshift meal, I dozed for a while, finally rousing myself just as *The Bill* was starting.

Feeling warm and cosy it would've been so easy to talk myself into abandoning my forthcoming enterprise, especially given the subject matter in *The Bill*. It was about victims taking matters into their own hands. No happy endings there. But there very rarely were in that particular programme. Then I thought about young Mark and his family, Jim's loss and my pain and humiliation, all of which went towards stiffening my resolve. After all this was real life, not some hour-long police soap opera.

The ringing of the phone roused me from my sombre reasonings. It was Greg. 'Hello, Tom. I don't know whether you've heard. Old Dean Martin was found dead this morning.'

'Oh dear, poor old fella.'

'He'll be missed around the Quays, especially in the cafe, smells and all.'

'Was it the booze or exposure that did it?'

'The general theory is exposure. His coat and boots were missing. The police think it was a falling out with another alky and Old Dean lost, hence the missing coat and boots. It must've been some row for him to lose both. Funny thing is his coat was found floating in the dock, that's probably where the boots are. Perhaps whoever he had the argument with just chucked them. Though it doesn't seem very rational for a plonky to dump a warm coat, but who am I to know the workings of their minds. I suppose you could say that by his standards Old Dean died a happy man. He was found with a bottle still clutched in his hand. Anyway, did Jane get off OK? I didn't interrupt a wild card party, did I?'

'I should be so lucky. The dog's not into strip poker. The flight left on time, which was something given the weather conditions. She'll have three weeks to get used to the warmth and sunshine before I arrive looking like the proverbial milk bottle. Anyway, thanks for letting me know about Old Dean. I bet Big Marge'll notice a difference in her disinfectant bills.' Greg laughed as we said goodbye. Thinking about Old Dean, I returned to the living room, wondering again what had happened in their lives that drove some folks to living rough.

At a quarter to eleven, I left the house clad in a dark jogging suit, black trainers and an old black duffle coat. A black balaclava stuffed in the pocket completed the outfit along with a pair of black gloves. My excuse in case I met any neighbours, was I was nipping down to the local off-licence, which didn't close until 11, for some cigarettes. Making my way out of the Close, I wasn't aware of any twitching curtains as I turned in the general direction of the Quays. Putting on my balaclava and pulling up my hood, I cut down back streets and side roads, keeping away from the main thoroughfares as much as possible.

I'd estimated that it'd take about 30 minutes to walk to my destination, but it wasn't far off half-eleven when I sidled into the alleyway by Greg's workshop. Entering at the furthest end from the cafe, I edged my way down keeping as close as possible to the wall, at the same time trying to still my laboured breathing caused through a combination of brisk walking and panic.

I was panicking in case someone caught me. What would I do or say! It'd appear very suspicious to be found lurking halfway down an entry, dressed all in black, on a bitterly cold night when most law-abiding citizens would be either snug and warm in front of the TV or cosily tucked up in bed. I suddenly smiled to myself and calmed down. If anyone saw me down here, it certainly wouldn't be any law-abiding citizen. It'd only be someone else going about their own bit of shady business.

Trying to relax, I longed for a smoke but knew that was the last thing I could do. Jumping, I tensed up again as something white rustled past my feet, before realising it was only a paper bag. The slight wind that blew used the alley as a funnel, blowing down the way I'd entered, through to the water. Water which I could hear ominously slap, slap, slapping against the quay wall.

I don't know how long I stood there but it seemed like an eternity. My initial warmth had all but dissipated and I tucked my hands under my arms which helped a little. But my feet were beginning to solidify inside my trainers, and I wondered if I'd be able to move at all when the time came.

Suddenly the reflected light from the cafe disappeared. I heard a car door slam, an engine start-up, and a vehicle drive off. *That must be Freddie, I can't have been down here as long as I imagined. I'm just so bloody cold.* These thoughts and any others I may have had on the matter of warmth or lack of were interrupted when the greyness at the end of the alley was momentarily darkened by a shadow. This shadow was closely followed by a second and then a third. The entrance became clear once more, and I could make out a huddled mass a couple of feet inside about five or six yards down from me.

'I've told you two time and time again, no goods or cash, no comestibles.'

Comestibles! What an odd word to use in the circumstances. It was the type of word that conjured up images of old-fashioned grocery shops, not dark and lonely alleys down on the docks. But there was nothing funny, humorous nor old-fashioned about the voice and I experienced a familiar prickle at the nape of my neck under my balaclava. I pressed myself even further against the wall. If I could make out their forms, surely they could make out mine! I fervently hoped not for that voice belonged to the third man from the cafe. The one in the voluminous scarf. None other than Arnold

Perry prize-winning poet of this parish. But this time his voice was so devoid of inflexion or feeling as to be colder than the night itself.

A whining sound came from one of the blurs. 'Ah come on, Muffler, you know we always turn up with the goods. When have we ever let you down?' It was a voice I hadn't heard before, so I surmised it belonged to Bobby. I wouldn't have put him down as a whiner.

'Frequently,' came the hissed whisper. 'But no more after tonight. Make do with what you've got. You'd also better produce what you owe me, plus more, by tomorrow night or you're both for the high jump. I've got my masters as well. Don't forget. Tomorrow night, half past ten in the cafe, and don't think you can escape me by not turning up. You won't. I know you two inside out, all your haunts and scams and all your little peccadillos. Be there.' With that, one of the shadows detached itself from the mass, covered the entrance for a second, and then was gone.

By now I could just discern Billy's blond head in the gloom, moving in rhythmic fashion. I surmised he was shivering, but whether from cold, fear or something else entirely I wasn't sure. He then spoke. 'What d'we do now, Bob?' He sniggered. 'Ah, forget Muffler. What does he know? Who does he think he is anyway? We haven't jumped anyone all week apart from Old Dean Martin last night, and we got nothing from him except a flea-ridden coat and a pair of old boots. Stupid bugger we wouldn't have taken them if he'd let go of that bottle.'

'*You* wouldn't you mean, I told you he wasn't worth bothering with.'

Billy carried on as if Bobby hadn't spoken. 'No one wants to be out in this, not walking the streets anyway. No little old ladies with their bingo winnings, not even any drunks going home from the pub.' His agitations were becoming more pronounced. 'Come on, I'm dying for a fix, hurry up and light the frigging joint.' As well as agitated, he sounded irritable and very peevish. No high-pitched giggle in evidence tonight.

I thought of the article I'd read at the dentist's. Was it only this morning! It seemed an eternity ago. Billy's immediate whim certainly wasn't being satisfied quickly enough for his liking, that much was evident.

'Wait your turn. It was my money that paid for it so I'm getting my fill first, you're like some snivelling little kid you are. Wait a minute will you or I'll duff you one and save Muffler the trouble.' There was no whine in Bobby's voice now, it must be switched on and off to suit his purpose.

'Yeah, your money. Who're you kidding? The stuff was paid for with dosh pinched from your old lady's purse.'

'Who cares where it came from, it was enough to buy a couple of joints wasn't it? But nowhere near enough to satisfy Muffler or pay back a fraction of what we owe him. I dunno what to do about him, he gives me the creeps. We can't just forget about him either. He'd find us no matter what.'

Bobby must have passed over the joint because I heard Billy take a couple of deep rasping breaths, dragging into his lungs whatever was in the cigarette as fast as he could. Whatever it was it worked pretty quickly for when he spoke again, he sounded calmer. His immediate whim had in fact been gratified.

'Oh, stuff Muffler, he doesn't frighten me. We can always get a new supplier who'll give us tick until we find more mugs or drunks.' His familiar giggle was back, which made the hairs on the back of my neck rise once more, but in an entirely different fashion to the way Muffler's had.

Whatever they were smoking was apparently not sufficient for Bobby's particular needs for his voice had become tight with tension. 'Come on, will you. I'm going home. I've got something hidden there, not as good but it'll work quicker from the needle. I need more than one sodding joint from friend sodding Muffler to get me going. I wish it wasn't so sodding cold. Sodding hurry up will you. You'd better doss down at ours because we've got to think of something to get Muffler his sodding dosh by tomorrow. I don't think it'd be wise to sodding cross him. I've known people just disappear. Remember Franky Forbes and Carl Williams? No one knows what happened to them, but the whisper is – Muffler. You'd be wise to be sodding frightened of him. Bloody hell, Billy, get your sodding finger out. Come on I'm sodding frozen.'

The mildness of the language surprised me somewhat. That one-word repetition almost like a child who's heard it somewhere, knows he shouldn't be repeating it, but does so for effect. I'm not sure what effect Bobby was after, perhaps his expletive supply was frozen as solid as he was – and me come to that.

As the two shadows detached themselves from the wall, one suddenly stopped and threw his arm up in the air. 'Yeah, I've got the sodding bloody answer.' It was Bobby.

'What to, Bob? Come on, I thought you were in a hurry.'

'Shut up, Billy, and listen to your Uncle Bobby. I know where I can get the money from.'

'Where? I'm too cold to break into anywhere tonight, Bob.'

'No, it's nothing like that. Shar.'

'Sharon! I thought you'd knocked that on the head.' There was surprise in Billy's voice.

'Oh, I have. But she'll do anything for me will Shar. Our problems with Muffler are over, Billy Boy. We don't have to see him until half-ten, so I'll get her to come down here about 10, give her a quick one and then go see Muffler. Come on, Billy, get a sodding move on.'

Movement, a momentary darkening and then the entrance to the alley was clear once more leaving me, a block of ice, still pressed against the wall and thinking with what small portion of my brain that hadn't yet solidified, that the joint hadn't improved Bobby's temperament one little bit. Even if he had solved his immediate financial problem.

Easing myself painfully away from the wall, I gingerly moved back up the entry the way I'd entered. Gingerly because I couldn't feel my hands or feet whatsoever so had to be careful I didn't bump into any unexpected obstacles, such as

wheelie bins or skips. I was halfway home before feeling began
to return to my feet. I was convincing myself that the throbbing
in my big toes was good when I slipped on a patch of black ice
and went down with a thud which jarred my whole body.
Cautiously picking myself up, I hobbled on my merry way
coming to the conclusion that I wasn't the total block of ice I
thought I was, judging by the smarting and aching that began
to make itself known to various parts of my body.

Hugging the hedges, I crept into the Close and edged
towards my gate, not remembering but praying I'd left it open,
and cursing under my breath for not oiling the hinges when
they first started squeaking. Fortunately, the gate was open,
and I'd also had the foresight to switch off the automatic
floodlight before leaving the house. Two brownie points to
me. Nevertheless, I sidled up the drive to the front door, which
I quietly opened and slipped inside without, I hope, making a
sound.

Standing in the hall, I rested my head against the door.
I was a mixture of aches, pains, cold and sweat, plus a whole
gamut of emotions. Relief, fear and hatred, with above all, an
iron determination to sort out those two little shits one way or
another. There was also the matter of poor Old Dean Martin's
death to be added to the list.

Locking the door, I went upstairs and ran a bath. As I lay
soaking, my body gradually thawing in the hot water, I contemplated my nocturnal activities. What had I achieved? Apart
that is from bruises and abrasions to both legs, a cut knee,
grazed elbows and hands, and feet frozen solid to the bone. I'd
ascertained that the two B's would be in the same place the following night, confirmation of which had been the aim of the
night's excursion. Plus, timing and secrecy.

Groaning, I heaved myself out of the bath, warmed through
but aching in every joint. I was also suddenly very hungry and
thirsty. Fishing out a pair of pyjamas, a reminder of my stay in
hospital, and donning my oldest but warmest dressing gown,
I returned downstairs.

Attempting to turf Charley out into the back garden was a total waste of time, and he didn't budge until I was making some corned beef sandwiches, then he was at my side in a flash. We shared the sandwiches but not the cocoa, and ruffling his head I thought that at his age he was entitled to conveniently ignore things he wasn't interested in. I really couldn't blame him for not wanting to go outside, as long as he didn't disturb me in the early hours.

Nursing my cocoa, I stared into the fire speculating on the make-up of Billy and Bobby and pondering on the article in the *Reader's Digest*. Hearing the hall clock strike two, I realised it was now Friday, that it'd been only yesterday I'd gone to the dentist. Thinking on all that had happened since then, I wondered how Jane was enjoying her flight and whether she was flying into dawn, dusk or sunshine. I shook my head. I was far too tired to work out times and distances but knew one thing, she'd be a darn sight warmer than I'd been a couple of hours ago.

I tried to drag my mind back to the learned article and if it applied to my two dregs of humanity, but my thoughts were too woolly, flitting here, there and everywhere. Giving up the struggle, I went to bed, hardly remembering my head touching the pillow.

Chapter Sixteen

Easing my back away from the iceberg that passed for a wall, I took a surreptitious glance at my watch. Nine forty-five. Was it only 10 minutes ago that I'd arrived in this dark, bleak alley?

The aches, pains and various bruises – legacies from the previous evening – had evidently been on hold for I don't remember being bothered by them on my walk to the Quays. On the other hand, perhaps they were frozen so solid they were anaesthetised. Attempting to flex my toes, I almost weakened asking myself again what on earth I was doing here; but then my resolve stiffened as the word 'REVENGE' began its repetitious hammering in my head.

Another 15 minutes at least before the unknown Shar was due to put in an appearance. I wondered just what her role was in Bobby's life and my thoughts returned to the previous evening and his oh so confident statement that Sharon would give him the money needed to pay Muffler.

Then I remembered with a start what else he'd said, which was to the effect that he'd give her a 'quick one' and it suddenly dawned on me what he meant. The cold must have closed down my brain cells for not cottoning on earlier what that implied. Time to retreat. But as I made to absent myself from a potentially embarrassing situation, there was movement at the entrance, and I literally froze, my back hard against the wall. Too late to disappear now.

I stood there pressed hard against the wall, rigid with a combination of fear, cold and acute embarrassment. The heat from the last emotion should've been enough to melt me on

SOFTLY TO THE QUAY

the spot. Amongst my other crimes, I'd now be able to add the one of voyeur. Not exactly a Peeping Tom for I wouldn't see anything if I tried, but definitely a Listening Leonard.

Two figures had moved up the alleyway and were standing behind a rubbish bin, not two yards away from me. A bead of sweat formed under the rim of my balaclava, and I battled to control my breathing. A third figure, Billy, stayed down near the entrance, continuously moving back and forth like a soldier on sentry duty.

The girl spoke. 'Does he have to be here, Bobby?' Her voice a combination of petulance and longing.

'He's the lookout, isn't he? We don't want anyone coming up here for a slash while we're in the middle of it, now do we?'

'Why've we got to do it here? Where've you been lately anyway? You promised you'd take me to yours to see your mother months ago. I don't see you for weeks and weeks and then all of a sudden you can't live without me – you can't go another day without having it away with me.'

'Shut up, Shar. I've told you over and over why I can't come to see you or take you to ours, me mam being sick and that. Now do you sodding well want it or not?' He was getting impatient.

'You know I do, Bobby. I'll do anything for you, you know that.' She giggled. 'It's so bleeding cold though, it's enough to freeze your balls off never mind a brass monkey's.'

'I'm warning you, Shar. Button it.'

'God it's freezing. I'm sure my arse is welded to this bloody wall. Why couldn't we go to my place, it's nice and warm there.'

'I've already told you, I don't know how many sodding times, I've got an important business appointment in half an hour. You live too sodding far away, I'd never get back in time.'

'We could've met earlier.'

'Oh, for Christ's sake, Shar, will you sodding well zip it.'

Sharon giggled again. 'If you don't unzip it, we won't get very far, will we?'

'I'll bloody well sock you one in a minute. Will you sodding well shut up before I gag you.'

Bobby's apparent agitation had transferred itself to his use of mild blasphemies just as it had the previous evening. Although it was hard to guess whether it was passion or impatience directing him at the moment. On my part, the words going through my mind were neither mild nor blasphemous, but they were definitely unrepeatable.

The short silence was suddenly broken by a rhythmic moaning from the girl accompanied by a deeper grunting from Bobby. Sweating with shame and mortification, I attempted to channel my thoughts elsewhere; anywhere except on the two people coupling almost within touching distance of my dark, acutely embarrassed form.

The girl spoke. 'Oh, Bobby, that was great. Now I know why I love you so much.'

'I love you as well, Shar, you know I do,' replied Bobby. Then almost in the same breath, 'Come on, hurry up, sort yourself out and give me the money, I've got to go.'

'You don't have to go right now, do you?' Sharon's mood changed and she sounded irritable. 'I'm sure we haven't been here half an hour. That didn't last five minutes, never mind thirty. Surely, it's not time yet for your so-called meeting. Aren't you even going to buy me a coffee from Freddie's?'

'Honest, Shar, there's no time. Besides, you know Freddie doesn't like females in the caff at night. He says they're only there to tout for business. It gives the place a bad name.' He sniggered. 'He's right, isn't he? Anyway, it's time you got back to your patch before some other scrubber nicks it.'

'You know I'd give up the game tomorrow for you.'

'Yeah. Well, as my old man used to say before he scarpered, I'll be OK when my ship comes in. Until then you'll have to keep doing your thing.' He sniggered again. 'Or getting your thing, as the case may be. I've really got to go, Shar, poor Billy must be iced through. He hasn't had you to warm him up. Ta for the money. I'll pay you back soon.'

'You always say that, but like everything else you never do. You must owe me hundreds by now. I'm beginning to think you only want me when you want money. I must be bloody stupid to keep coming back for more, but it never fails does it. Bobby cocks his finger, amongst other things, and silly, stupid Sharon always comes running.'

'Don't be like that, Shar, it only seems that way. You know there've been plenty of times when I haven't had any money off you.'

'When? The only time was probably the first time we had it off, the first time we met. How old was I? About 14 if I remember rightly. I don't suppose I had any money to give you then, otherwise you'd have had that as well as me. Full of promises you are, Bobby. All of them as empty as that stupid Billy's head. I don't know why I keep coming back for more. I must be as stupid as him. Each time this happens I tell myself that's it, enough's enough. Then you turn up again and I fall every time. I need my bloody head examining.'

'Oh, Shar, come on, forget the money issue. You know I love you, and I've told you time and time again why I can't take you home just yet. I've got to break it gently to the old girl that we're serious. I can't do that when she's so sick can I?' His voice changed from the wheedling and conciliatory to disgust. 'Ah you're not whingeing, are you? I can't stand whingeing females. I'm off. Ta again for the dosh. See ya.' Bobby moved off towards Billy then they both disappeared, leaving Sharon to make her own way out. For one awful moment, I thought she might decide to leave via me. Fortunately for the benefit of both our blood pressures and after some sniffling and muttering of 'bastard, bastard, bastard', she tottered off in their wake. Her high heels click-clacking down the entry until she too disappeared into the night.

Slowly relaxing from my rigid stance, I took a deep breath. I'm sure I'd not breathed since entering the alley which must have been hours ago. It was an effort to lift my arm, but I managed it and looked at my watch in disbelief.

That sordid little interlude had taken all of 15 minutes but, and it was a very big but, it'd take an awful lot longer than that before the shame and guilt left me.

So, Bobby had got his money to pay off Muffler. Although the callous and cold-hearted way he'd got it only emphasised his insensitive egocentric personality. Irrespective of Sharon's "profession" the poor bitch deserved better from her so-called "lover". That little performance by Bobby was just another nail in his coffin as far as I was concerned. I was in no mood to hang around any longer. Enough was enough for one night. I turned my tired feet towards home. Mentally exhausted, emotionally nauseated, physically cold and weary to the very bone.

Chapter Seventeen

I awoke late the next morning, stiff and sore, wincing as I turned over to look at the clock. The little red face showed it was well gone eight, which surprised me somewhat for I thought I'd have been awake much earlier after a restless night. But judging by the neatness of the duvet it appeared I'd slept the sleep of the just and hardly moved a muscle.

The muscles had to be moved now, however. Making my aching way to the bathroom, I grunted and groaned with every step, something I would've had to do in silence if Jane were here. It was almost an hour later before I finally left the house after having a bite to eat and taking Charley for a crawl around the block.

Short though it was, the walk did me good and eased some of the stiffness from my legs and shins, both of which were very sore to touch. Time for a massage with Deep Heat or Dog Oil. The former had a more inspiring name but a strong smell, while the latter with the awful name had no smell whatsoever. In fact, I used neither and went off to work, sore limbs untouched by any soothing balm, smelly or otherwise.

At the office, I managed to get through quite a lot of necessary paperwork and telephone calls, keeping my mind so occupied with business that I barely had time for any passing thoughts on the previous evening. The odd time it did cross my mind, embarrassment and shame washed over me, and I was thankful to be alone in the office.

I also pitied that poor cow Sharon. She was just as much Bobby's victim as Mark or myself. He used and abused her with total disregard for any finer feelings she might have once possessed. He wanted something, she had it, so he took it. He just changed his methods to suit his victims.

Jeff and I called it a day around half four, quite satisfied by the amount of work we'd achieved. Saying goodbye, we went our separate ways through the darkness and the sparse early Saturday evening traffic. The threatened rain had held off, but it was still bitterly cold, and I was glad to get indoors.

The dog made such a fuss when I greeted him, I felt guilty of desertion, which was his intention. To ease my conscience, I took him for a quick walk before feeding us both. He then settled himself before the fire effectively cutting me off from the direct heat. He sure knows how to get his own back. I left him there thinking he'd move when he became too hot, but from the contented sighs emanating from his supine form, I changed my mind – he was there for the night.

Trying to concentrate on the television was nigh on impossible. I was looking and listening, but nothing was going in. The lottery results came and went. My name could have been spelt out in yard high lights as a potential millionaire it still wouldn't have registered. My mind was on other things. Attempts to read the evening paper were also a waste of time so I gave up and let my thoughts drift where they would, namely the cause of my old and new bruises. Billy and Bobby.

I saw them not as two individuals but as a pair of thugs. Siamese twin ne'er-do-wells. One unable to operate without the other, a scumbag double act, totally selfish and unprincipled, operating in tandem. Were they two ideal candidates for the psychologists' theory of delinquency? I wasn't in a position to know if they'd been over-indulged and spoiled as children, but the signs pointed that way. I could say with some degree of certainty, they didn't qualify for the second theory – deprived and neglected childhoods. Not if "call me Brenda" was anything to go by. Nor the furore generated by Bobby's mother in trying to cover up his attempted burglary. Perhaps they'd both been born jerks, defective genes, bad seeds, or some other inbred moral deficiency.

Musing on these and other random thoughts, I stared vacantly into space until the chiming of the hall clock roused me from my lethargy. Sighing, I went to make ready for my now familiar walk to the Quays. I had a large whisky, kidding myself that it was for warmth but knowing full well it was for Dutch courage.

Leaving the house much later than the previous evening, I gave an involuntary shiver as the cold hit me like a slap in the face, momentarily stopping me dead in my tracks. I wasn't wearing the duffle coat this time around. Instead, I wore a lightweight sweater under my tracksuit top, over which I'd put on an old black jumper and one of those thick sleeveless waistcoats. Two pairs of tracksuit bottoms and two pairs of socks completed the thermal ensemble. On top of this lot, I wore a black pacamac, plus of course my balaclava and gloves. The overall effect felt like the Michelin tyre man out for an evening roll and I fervently hoped no one was about who knew me.

It was 11pm when I entered the alleyway, and in the distance, I could hear the town hall clock chiming the hour. "Ask not for whom the bell tolls." I hadn't seen another soul on my walk to the Quay. If I'd passed anyone, I hadn't been aware of them, and there'd been very little traffic on the roads. This surprised me in one way because it was the weekend, but not in another for there'd been a severe gale warning for this area. That much at least had registered from the television.

There'd been no noticeable increase in the wind on my walk, but I'd kept to the more sheltered side streets as much as possible. But even here at the quayside there was only a brief flurry or occasional gust of wind, although these had a promise of more to come.

Walking the length of the alley, I found what I was looking for, a couple of waste bins next to a wheelie bin. Inverting one lid, I placed one bin on top of the other; fortunately, neither was overfull but had just enough rubbish in both to keep them steady. As quietly as possible, I moved the wheelie bin a little way towards the others and then squeezed in the gap between the two lots of bins.

This was my temporary cover. There was no plan.

I didn't even know what I'd do if both Billy and Bobby came into the entry together. I was reckoning on past observations that for some reason of their own, first one, usually Bobby, would enter followed a couple of minutes later by the other. I was barely in time for no sooner had I positioned myself when Bobby arrived and leant against the wall. My nerve almost deserted me. I froze and would've held back except I saw him swinging a short stubby cosh on a leather strap. Back and forth, back and forth it swung like the rhythmic movements of a pendulum. I recalled once again the pain and anguish of the attack, the force of each blow. Back and forth, back and forth went the cosh. My blood began to boil. The vengeful side of me took over, and I walked from behind those bins carrying a brick, which for the life of me I didn't remember picking up. I must have made a slight noise for Bobby was in the act of turning towards me when the brick caught him on the back of the head.

He went down in slow motion, more of a crumble than a fall. Catching him before he hit the ground, I dragged him to a sitting position against the wall, hoping he'd remain unconscious. Retrieving the brick, I retreated behind my metal cover and waited. Sweat ran into my eyes in total contradiction to the coldness of the night, and I was shaking all over.

When Billy arrived, it was a second or two before he noticed Bobby propped against the wall. But then he did exactly what I hoped. He went to him, leant down, shook him and called his name.

'Bobby, what's up with you then? Been mixing it without me, or have you used my share? Ah come on, Bob, stop playing round. I'm getting bloody desperate here.' He shook Bobby again, this time much more violently. He was becoming agitated, and I fully expected him to start giggling and skip up and down the entry. Waiting no longer, I stepped from behind my cover before he could straighten up. With my right hand, I plunged the knife under his left shoulder blade, the point of the stiletto angling towards and finding his heart. A faint gasp of surprised breath was all the noise he made. He might have been dead before he even reached the ground.

The hardest part was removing the knife. Taking a deep breath, I pulled. It was wet and sticky as I placed it in Bobby's right hand, he was still holding on to the cosh with his left. With shaking hands, I took out the second knife to use on Bobby. I couldn't do it. I stood there for an eternity, trembling and sweating. Nausea washed over me in waves as I looked at the two bodies at my feet. Looking but not seeing.

Bobby groaned; he was coming round. He mustn't see me. I began to turn away. Too late. Bemused and confused as he was, Bobby gave a strangled cry and swung the cosh catching me across the knees. I reacted instantly. Fear coupled with hate and loathing impelled me forward, and I buried the knife into his neck where it joined the shoulder. A gurgling rattle and then nothing.

For a split second, I stared at them both in horror before galvanising myself into action, expecting at any moment to be discovered. Tentatively, I searched Bobby's pockets, finding several small packets of what I assumed to be dope, returning all except for a couple, which I dropped by the bins. I then dragged Billy's body and laid it across Bobby's, before finally wrapping his hand around the knife where it protruded from Bobby's neck.

The picture was complete. 'Is there anything I've forgotten,' I muttered casting around with a small pencil torch. Checking there were no footprints or other incriminating evidence in the blood – of which to my surprise there appeared to be very little. After carefully rearranging the bins to their original positions, I made my way from the entry the same way I'd entered.

I turned my footsteps towards home, but my legs didn't want to respond as they should. It wasn't the blow from the cosh, although I was very conscious of my throbbing knees, which together with the bruises from Thursday evening, did nothing to help my progress. No, it was as if my legs were out of synchronisation with the rest of my body, especially my mind, and I stumbled and weaved like a drunken man.

I couldn't think straight. Couldn't even walk straight and I felt very, very sick. The next minute I was retching, but there was no relief, even after leaving the contents of my stomach in the gutter. A passing police car would surely pick me up for being drunk and incapable. If that happened, considering the state I was in, I'd have confessed right away that I'd just carried out a double murder.

Fortunately, there were no passing police cars, no passing traffic at all on the short stretch of main road I had to negotiate before reaching the side roads and back streets. I tried to be as inconspicuous as possible, but with my ungainly staggering progression, I had the impression whole neighbourhoods were following my stumbling, halting footsteps. And were clamouring at the top of their voices, shouting to the rooftops that I was a foul fiend. A murderer.

It was getting harder and harder to put one foot in front of the other as if I were straining against an invisible barrier. A barrier intent on sending me back to the scene of my crime. The thought of instant retribution flashed through my mind as unseen hands pushed me with such force that I was propelled backwards for several yards before my feet were lifted from under me and I was flung hard against a wall.

I landed with a thud on the ground, where, before I could even draw breath, a malevolent being was intent on hammering me into the wall to become one with the brickwork. A sudden lull in the noise and clamour enabled me to greedily gulp in lungfuls of air as the force eased its weight off my chest. Breathing heavily, too frightened to move, I rested against the wall attempting to grasp at my disorientated thoughts.

Eventually, I realised the malign being wasn't a demon conjured up by the ghosts of Billy and Bobby. Neither was it a figment of my deranged imagination, although it might well have been, considering the state I was in. It finally penetrated what passed for my brain that it was, in fact, the promised gale. One up to the weathermen. I didn't have a clue what strength it was but for one fleeting moment was glad I wasn't on the high seas.

Pulling myself to my feet, I ignored the mass of aches and pains that demanded attention. As long as I could walk in whatever manner, I was going home.

I don't know how long I'd been sitting on the ground, or for how long the lull had lasted, it seemed like hours but from recent experience, I guessed it to be only a few seconds and wouldn't last many more. In this I was right. No sooner had I started on my way than the banshees recommenced their cat-erwauling around the chimney pots, and invisible hands were once again intent on grinding me into the ground. This time I was prepared and was able to make progress, be it at a snail's pace. A very old, slow snail to boot.

It was a nightmare journey. I was buffeted and blown from side to side, flung backwards and forwards, and tossed into the gutter like a piece of rubbish. But still I pushed steadily forward. All thoughts of Billy, Bobby and what had happened at the Quay totally erased from my mind. Survival was now my main priority, and I was having an almighty battle. Then came the rain. It started in one of the infrequent lulls, dropping like icicles, painful, hard and icy cold. By this time, I was past caring. My only aim was to get to my front door – hopefully in one piece.

I trudged on through the wind, rain, squalls, hailstones, falling slates and chimney pots. Wheelie bins came at me like vengeful steamrollers, rubbish flying everywhere as they clattered and careered past; while milk bottles bounced on doorsteps before they too were tossed aside to smash into so many broken shards. Branches smacked me in the face as they were torn from trees and in the distance, I heard a mighty groan as some great tree was uprooted, torn down by the storm like something of no significance.

This was on the periphery of my senses, for I needed all my concentration and strength to inch my way forward as well as trying to breathe. For every three breaths, the wind snatched two away. Attempting to breathe by gulping air in short, shallow bursts left me gasping and wheezing, something akin to Greg's Flora on its first outing.

Eventually, I made it to the Close and, although the wind still howled and the rain battered down, I was able to move in a reasonably upright position. But I still instinctively hugged the hedges. It wouldn't have mattered, however, had I danced and sung stark naked up and down the middle of the road. No one would have heard me above the noise of that storm. Or seen me either for there wasn't one single light to be seen in the whole of the Close.

Still hugging the privet, I made it to the front door. With my back to the elements that had tried so hard to break me, I carefully fished out the key from where I'd hidden it earlier. It was pitch black, and barely able to control my shaking hands, it took several attempts before I finally managed to locate the keyhole.

Turning the key, I pushed open the door and lurched rather than stepped into the hall, the comparative quietness of which was as disorientating in its own way as the almighty cacophony outside.

Chapter Eighteen

The door closed behind me. Leaning against it, I slowly regained my breath. This became less ragged, but my whole body was trembling so much I did the only sensible thing under the circumstances and slid down until I was sitting on the floor, my back resting against the door. For the time being at least, I'd reached the end of my endurance.

I sat there for I don't know how long, shaking, trembling and gasping, before slowly becoming aware that another sensation was trying to make itself known to me. I located this feeling to my left hand, which was clenched so tightly my nails were digging into my palm. Painfully and with some difficulty I prised open my fingers one by one and found a small round object nestling in my palm.

Turning it over and over as my rasping breath slowly quietened, I became conscious of two things. Firstly, this small round object was a button, presumably from the mac I was no longer wearing, and secondly, it had been clenched in my bare hand. What on earth had happened to the raincoat and gloves? I shook my head in stupefaction, which was a big, big mistake. Where the pain began or ended was a sealed envelope from then on. From the top of my head right down to my toes, my whole being ached, throbbed and stung.

Unable to even begin to think coherently, I dragged myself up from the floor and shambled towards the kitchen, fumbling for the light switch as I went. Nothing happened. Power failure. That explained why the Close was in darkness. Locating the stairs, I crawled on my hands and knees up to the bathroom. My eyes gradually becoming used to the darkness, a darkness punctuated by occasional flashes of lightning along with extremely loud thunder.

Clumsily and with great difficulty, I managed to turn on the bath taps and strip off what was left of my torn and sodden clothing. With even greater difficulty, I levered myself into the hot water into which I'd thrown (I hoped) bath salts, bubble bath and whatever else was to hand. Lying back, I closed my eyes. Still without any coherent thoughts, I let the water ease my battered and bruised body, and the heat soak through my pores in the hope it'd melt the block of ice that used to be Tom Marshall. The storm seemed to increase in intensity if that was at all possible, and in a vague sort of way I wondered if we'd lose many slates or worse the roof and chimney pots.

A particularly loud clap of thunder accompanied by a continuous ringing roused me with a start. I must have dozed off for the water had cooled considerably and I was beginning to shiver again.

'Brr-brr, brr-brr, brr-brr.'

'Whoever that is at the door,' I muttered to the gloom, 'I wish to hell they'd go away.'

'Brr-brr, brr-brr, brr-brr.'

Then the penny dropped. If there was no electricity, there was no doorbell ringing. That rhythmic noise pounding like a sledgehammer in my head was the telephone, and whoever was calling wasn't going to go away.

'Brr-brr, brr-brr, brr-brr.'

Cursing, I heaved myself out of the water, making a grab for what I hoped was the towel rail and a towel, banging my shins on the side of the bath in the process. Bruises on bruises on bruises. Convinced I had two broken legs, I shuffled and felt my way along the murk of the landing to the bedroom.

'Brr-brr, brr-brr, brr-brr.'

Would the bloody thing never stop! I was at screaming point by the time I located the phone, almost knocking it to the floor in my haste to stop the incessant ringing. But it didn't stop.

'Brr-brr, brr-brr, brr-brr.'

The phone in my hand was dead. It stood to reason that the phone lines as well as the power would be down.

'Brr-brr, brr-brr, brr-brr.'

My mobile, of course. I hadn't risked taking it out with me. But where had I left it? Fumbling about I found it on the dressing table. If I'd been in any fit state to even wonder who'd be calling at this late hour, I'd automatically have assumed it was Jane, although she'd be hard put to phone from 33,000ft high. Naturally, it wasn't Jane. In fact, the person at the other end was the total antithesis to my beloved wife.

The voice belonged to no other than Muffler. The late Billy and Bobby's mentor. Or to give him his proper title Mr Arnold Perry (prize-winning poet of this parish).

He spoke, or rather hissed in that chilling tone of his, only a few simple words before the line went dead.

'I know. I saw you. I'll be in touch.'

I sat on the bed unable to move a muscle, phone still clutched in my hand. Aches, pains, bruises, screaming headache, everything forgotten except for that voice and those few simple words. Eventually, I roused myself as some semblance of cognitive thinking finally crept into my dulled senses. 'Are you going to sit there forever like the sphinx with that damned phone in your hand, Tom!'

I spoke aloud for two reasons. One was to give myself courage, and the other was to hear the sound of another human voice (even if it was my own). Anything to drown out the memory of Muffler's words, which had found room in my aching head to hammer away along with everything else, as persistently as the ringing of the phone.

'Right, Tom, you can either stare into space until daylight, thinking of nothing or everything, and drive yourself mad, or do something positive and go downstairs and get a drink. Now isn't the time for retrospective recriminations. The hows, the whys, the guilt, or lack thereof. And now certainly isn't the time to worry about the hows or whys of Mr Arnold Perry.'

Standing up was an effort, but I managed it in the end and found a torch in the bedside cabinet (my pencil flashlight having gone the way of the gloves and mac). I was shivering again. Probably a combination of cold and shock but I was also stark naked apart from a damp towel. Rummaging around for pyjamas and slippers and grabbing my dressing gown from behind the door, I slowly and painfully made my way downstairs.

The clock in the hall chimed three as I passed. The chimes competing with the storm outside and the one inside my head. In the kitchen, I could vaguely see the outline of the dog in his basket. He wasn't moving, which meant he had his paws over his head, his favourite position when he doesn't want to be disturbed. I certainly wasn't going to disturb him.

Fortunately, we have a gas cooker, so I was able to heat some milk, letting it boil over in the process. Liberally laced with whisky, I drank it as quickly as I could and repeated the process. Successfully this time. Adding even more whisky, I also swallowed four pain killers for good measure. Stumbling up the stairs once more, I fell into bed.

Before sleep overtook me something that had been nagging at me, from the tiny recess of my brain that was still functioning, finally surfaced. How had Muffler got hold of my mobile phone number! That question would have to wait.

Tonight, I needed oblivion.

Chapter Nineteen

Having been granted my few hours of oblivion, I was very reluctant to emerge from my deep, dreamless sleep. But emerge I did by being rudely awakened by a furious hammering on the front door.

Being woken like that was both confusing and terrifying. Confusing because I was unable for a moment to pinpoint what was different, before it came to me that, apart from the hammering on the door, it was relatively quiet outside. The wind was still howling, and the rain still battered down but without the force or ferocity of the previous night. And terrifying because the memory and enormity of what I'd done, plus the phone call, came back with a rush and I went rigid with fear.

It must be Muffler who was hammering non-stop at the door, just as he had telephoned non-stop last night. Perhaps the police were with him.

'Tom. Tom. Are you awake? Tom.'

I knew that voice. It was neither the police come to arrest me, nor Muffler, but my neighbour Bill Gibbons. Moving my head to look at the clock, I shouted with pain as the pincers tightened on the back of my neck. Movement of any sort was a mistake for it set off every other ache, pain and spasm in my body. There wasn't a single part of me that didn't hurt (or so it seemed). But I had to make a move. As well as Bill outside, Charley was whimpering to be let out.

It was no good lying there, I had to move. For one thing it was necessary to behave in as normal a manner as possible, checking for damage to the house and garden and communing and commiserating with my neighbours. Wincing with every movement, I struggled out of bed and hobbled across to the window but couldn't even find the strength to open it. Miming to Bill that I'd be down shortly, he pointed to his watch and held up both hands from which I surmised he'd return in about 10 minutes.

Ten minutes. Very little time to get myself into some sort of working order, but it'd have to do. First things first. I had to see to the dog, who must have all four legs crossed judging by the whining which was getting louder and louder by the minute. Gingerly putting on my dressing gown, I eased my way along the landing to the stairs which appeared as long and as steep as a descent from Everest.

Negotiating them was an agonising nightmare to say nothing of stretching up to unlock the kitchen door for Charley, who hardly waited for it to be opened before shooting through like a shot from a cannon. I stood there in a daze, undecided what to do next. Take pain killers? Attempt to get dressed? See to my cuts and bruises? Check if anything was broken? I hadn't the foggiest idea how I looked.

Oh God, too late now. There was Bill hammering at the door again. At least I hoped it was him.

'Dear Jesus, Tom. What happened to you?'

Well now I had an inkling of how bad I was.

Bill continued, 'You weren't out in that lot last night, were you?'

Declining not to answer his question I replied, 'You don't look too good yourself, Bill.'

'I guess not but hope I don't look as bad as you.' Fortunately, he didn't press for an explanation but laughed. 'I don't think anyone had much beauty sleep last night. Boy, what a storm. Anyway, as the electricity's still off, Pam's doing breakfasts for all and sundry. She's set up her version of a soup kitchen in the caravan, which I'm pleased and surprised to say is still standing in one piece. Half the Close are already over there.'

'Thanks, Bill, but I'll be fine. We've got gas. In fact, the overflow could come over here.' As I spoke, I fervently hoped no one would take up the offer.

'Fraid that won't do as an excuse,' said Bill. 'Pam was insistent that you come, she thinks you'll starve to death without Jane. Fortunately, all the kids seem to want are cornflakes and toast. Now the storm's abated it's one big adventure to them.' He gestured around him. 'No adventure for us though, just look at the mess, and we're reasonably sheltered here. At least the rain's finally eased up.'

'I suppose we should be grateful for small mercies but that lot's going to take some clearing up, isn't it? Good job it's Sunday. Should I bring some eggs and bacon over? I know we've got plenty of sausages in the freezer.' A sudden thought hit me. 'Oh shit, the freezer. It's packed to the hilt. Jane was making sure I wouldn't go short. Good thing it is full, not so much chance of defrosting. Perhaps we won't have sausages after all.'

Bill nodded. 'The food should be OK for about 12 hours, especially if the freezers aren't opened. But if the power isn't back on by then, well, matey, we'll be queuing up at the homes of all you gas cooker owners with our sides of lamb and defrosted chips.'

I managed to smile with him. It was painful and felt more like a grimace, but I did it. 'I'll be over shortly, Bill.' I rubbed my chin, another mistake. 'I need a shave amongst other things and have to check the house isn't in imminent danger of falling down around me.'

'Right. Don't forget to do something about that black eye too. Pity all the steaks are frozen. See you later. Don't be too long or Pam'll send the troops over in force.'

Closing the door behind him, I looked in the hall mirror. Was that mess of a face mine? How would I explain that away to the neighbours? By now, Bill would have told them all I was sporting a shiner. Sighing I went through to the kitchen to let the dog in and noticed for the first time the devastation in the garden. I stood aghast, glad that Jane wasn't there to see the mess. The garden was her pride and joy. But now, as well as uprooted bushes and shrubs all over the place and the greenhouse in smithereens, there was a strange shed sitting rather lopsidedly in the middle of the lawn.

There was the answer to my black eye. Smashed in the face by a gate-crashing shed. It could very well have been the truth. This wasn't the time for flippancy, though I could put that down to a few loose brain cells I was sure were rattling around in my head.

I quickly shut the door; the garden would have to wait. My immediate priority was painkillers – extra strong. My neck and shoulders were having a competition as to which part could hurt the most, at the same time sending excruciating stabs of pain through my skull. Idly wondering if I had concussion again, I contemplated taking four tablets but settled for three washed down with some milk. There was a puddle on the floor, the fridge defrosting, which in turn reminded me of my torn and sodden clothing still lying on the bathroom floor. All that, however, would have to wait. I had to get dressed and manoeuvre myself across the road.

Once again, I painfully negotiated the stairs and spent what seemed hours dabbing various cuts and scratches with antiseptic, sticking plasters on the worst cuts and rubbing balm into my many bruises, aches and pains. I had a shave, which though painful, made me feel and look a little more presentable. There wasn't much I could do about the black eye. Considering the state the rest of my body was in, due in no small part to the frequent contact I'd made with walls pavements and Bobby's cosh, my hands were only slightly lacerated. Thus, I was able to present some semblance of normality when I finally limped across for breakfast.

The children, fascinated by my black eye, made my lies easier to tell, especially our three-year-old Godchild, Jennifer. I told them Doctor Who's Tardis had appeared in our back garden in the middle of the storm and the door had hit me in the eye when it opened. Even though Doctor Who was lost on the younger ones, they all found it hilarious, so it was no big step from that story to the one about a plank from the flying garden shed hitting me instead. My story was accepted at face value, probably because a garden shed was only one of the many unusual things flying around last night, many of which I could personally vouch for.

Everyone had stories to tell. What happened when this went bang, whether they screamed when that crashed, and how they felt when they thought the house would be blown away. How frightened they were, how the children reacted. My fabricated tale was just one of the many and was soon lost in the general discussion of the storm. I idly wondered how they'd react if I told the truth about how I got my black eye; although by now I was beginning to wonder if the whole thing wasn't some figment of my overwrought imagination.

It was while munching my way through a mixed grill, minus sausages, glad to be out of the house, and for the moment Muffler's reach (imagined or otherwise), that I learnt the power had gone off around half past one but no one knew at what time the telephone lines had gone down. However, Laura Smith said that according to the local radio the electricity was due to be restored "any time now", but she didn't know about the telephone lines.

I also learnt it had been a freak storm of such intensity there were no previous records, and the main force had been concentrated in this area of the country. Roofs, chimneys, trees and even walls had been blown down. Streetlamps, traffic lights, anything moving or otherwise had been blown down or away by the force of the storm.

I was digesting this information along with my food, thinking I was probably lucky to be alive when Laura said, 'And three bodies have been fished out of the dock.'

This last piece of news gave me such a jolt I choked on my tea, but, as I was being thumped on the back, old Mr Reynolds called to say the electricity was back on and in the general exodus, Laura's announcement was temporarily forgotten.

A short time later I too made my way home, trying not to limp and doing my best to walk upright, although as it was still very windy, I think I could be excused in the circumstances. Even though the breakfast and the pills had helped somewhat, I swallowed another couple of pills to keep the worst of the agony at bay. Ignoring the accusing looks from the dog (what did he know!), I managed to sort out the fridge, check the freezer, re-set the clocks, surprised to find it was still only half-ten, and do various other small jobs without actually shouting out in pain.

Checking the phone, still dead, I did a snail's climb up to the bathroom and contemplated the soggy mess of clothing still lying in a heap. How to get rid of them! I smiled; it couldn't be better. No one'd be the slightest bit interested – not today of all days. Everyone would be far too busy clearing up their own debris to be concerned over a few wet rags even if they noticed them.

Shoving the clothes into a bin liner, I came across the button and with it the memory that this was all that was left of the waterproof. Where were the gloves? The only conclusion I came to, was that the mac had been ripped to shreds and blown away and I must have removed the gloves for some reason and then lost them, or they too had been blown away. I'm certain I was still wearing both when I left the alleyway. Only mildly bothered, perhaps as a result of all the painkillers, I idly wondered if they could be traced to me and if they'd be incriminating. I gave an involuntary shudder. The gloves were totally irrelevant with Muffler in the background.

The actual deed had been pushed to the back of my mind. I had made a conscious effort not to think of what I'd done – which was premeditated murder. I wasn't ready yet to face my conscience, the reason I hadn't turned on the radio to listen to the news. Unfortunately, if I'd shoved the deed to the back of my mind, Muffler's words flatly refused to go away.

I could still hear his voice. 'I know. I saw you. I was there.' How had he known? I hadn't seen him. But then after my initial fear of discovery, I hadn't looked. My only aim had been to leave the scene as quickly as possible. He'd known who I was. How? From the cafe or Greg's? The Poetry Awards? How did he get my mobile phone number? It didn't really matter how – he knew, and that apparently was enough for Muffler.

Sitting on the edge of the bath, I contemplated what I'd do when Muffler next made contact. What would he want? It wouldn't be legitimate; otherwise the police would already be here. The only conclusion I could logically come to was blackmail. I'd go to the police myself before I paid anything to that creep. But until, and unless, Mr Arnold Perry (Poet) made contact again, I wasn't going to do a damn thing about it.

Wincing with every step, I carried the bag downstairs, and groaning with pain, rummaged under the sink for more bin bags and went out to join the rest of the Close in clearing up the roadway, pavements and drives as best we could. It was rather like a paper chase, for although the rain had ceased, it was still blowing a gale.

A couple of hours of backbreaking work left me no time to worry about the events of the previous night even if I'd been of a mind to but was instead a constant reminder of my aches and pains. A small mountain of refuse sacks was piled up at the end of the road ready for the tip. Driveways were clear, broken fences stacked neatly on one side, shattered glass gathered up, roof tiles heaped all together, and every household was once more in possession of a wheelie bin. Fortunately, no one had lost a chimney, and no one claimed the stray garden shed on my lawn, so I left it where it was for the moment.

Retiring once more to the area around Pam's caravan, we thankfully tucked into tea and scones, rustled up by one of the elderly neighbours, all other able-bodied folk had been recruited for manual labour. The children were hoping their various schools had been blown away and were getting quite excited at the thought of an enforced holiday.

Laura soon put a damper on those hopes. The latest news bulletin stated there'd been no major structural damage in our area. 'Unless we hear any different, it's school as usual tomorrow for you three,' she told her boys. Their crestfallen faces had us laughing, but they weren't down for long and were soon clamouring to be allowed to accompany the adults to the local refuse tips.

'Well, you've all worked as long and hard as the rest of us, so there's no reason why you can't,' said their father. 'You might as well finish the job off properly and help get rid of the sacks.'

Eight-year-old Paul came with me, and once the boot and back seat were filled to overflowing with sacks and boxes, we set off, although not before I'd nipped home for another three painkillers. (If anyone were to shake me, I'm sure I'd rattle.) I checked my mobile. No messages, thank God. I left it behind. Out of sight, out of mind. In theory anyway. Via Laura and her radio, we knew all three dumps were open and I opted for the one furthest away, using the argument that most people from this area would make for the nearest, which just happened to be situated near the docks and they'd have to queue for ages. The real reason was, I had no desire to visit any docks whatsoever, whether they were near the scene of my crime or otherwise.

We were soon part of a long queue ourselves, all crawling towards the same place. Crawling was the only sensible way forward due to the negotiating needed to avoid all the debris scattered on the roads. Trees, some of which had been dragged to one side, several overturned cars, two lamp-posts leaning drunkenly into the road (I was extra careful passing them), glass all over the place and, most incongruous of all, a washing machine sitting in the middle of a roundabout. I wondered if it was a kindred spirit to the wayward shed in my garden. Such thoughts as these, taking into account all that had happened in the last 15 hours or so, made me feel like a character in some surreal, macabre farce.

'D'you think that washing machine came out of a house, Uncle Tom?' asked Paul as we passed. 'If it did the whole house must've been blown away. It's just like *The Wizard of Oz,* isn't it?'

'More likely to have been on a wagon or in someone's garden or yard. But how it finished up over there is anyone's guess,' I said, carefully negotiating another hazard. 'Were you very frightened last night?'

'Well.' Paul paused. 'I was really but didn't say anything at first because of Julie. She's only four and she was very scared. I wasn't half glad when we got into Mum and Dad's bed. We were all squashed, but it was better than being on my own. I think I was more frightened because it was so noisy and dark except for the lightning.'

I knew what he meant. I too had been very frightened last night. Before the storm when I was in that entry, and later on my way home, I'd been assailed by two different kinds of fear. Fear of discovery and fear for my life. I was still experiencing the first. But just looking at the amount of debris on this one road, I suppose I was lucky not to have been seriously injured or even killed. The latter would certainly have made an ironic ending to my evening's activities.

Waiting in the line of cars and vans at the turn off to the tip, I switched on the radio without thinking and caught the end of the three o'clock news bulletin.

'... the three bodies taken from the dock at Queensway Quay have now been identified but are not being named until the next of kin have been notified. The cause of death is not yet known. Our next bulletin will be at three-thirty when there will be an update on the storm and its aftermath. Now back to Dave Meredith and his music.'

I turned the sound down as Paul said, 'I wonder if they'd been fishing and were blown in by the wind or pulled in by a big fish. A shark or something. I expect they were three men, don't you, Uncle Tom? Girls wouldn't go fishing in the dark, would they?'

I smiled as I answered, 'I don't think you'd find a shark in the docks, Paul. Not these docks anyway and yes, some girls and ladies do go fishing at night. But we'll have to wait a little longer to find out whether they were men or women, or how they got into the water.'

What had happened to the bodies of Billy and Bobby? Were they still in the alleyway waiting to be discovered? Surely not! Not with all the police activity that would've been going on down in that area all day. If they were two of the three in the dock, how had they got there and who was the third? If not, had there been another killer down that way last night or was it an accident? Two murderers operating in the same vicinity on the same night was too far-fetched, even for my imagination.

My head began to throb with these unbidden thoughts I was having to acknowledge. My right knee was stiffening up, not to mention all the other aches and pains shouting for attention. (The numbing effect of the pills wasn't lasting very long.) My head whirled, and I thought I was going to faint. While I'd been busy, I'd pushed unwelcome and un-wanted thoughts to one side, but now sitting here in this line of cars, reaction was setting in. Perhaps I was also suffering from delayed shock. I felt sick at the enormity of what I'd done. I broke out in a cold sweat and my hands began to shake. Taking several deep breaths, I gripped the steering wheel a little tighter, hoping young Paul wouldn't notice any-thing amiss.

Fortunately, at that moment, the traffic started to move forward, and we were in the next batch to go through to the skips. Thus, the manoeuvring, stopping, unloading and heaving the rubbish into the skips, along with the cold air, was enough to clear my head – for a while at least. Although sitting for so long in the car, all my other pains were complaining at having this enforced activity thrust on them once more.

Council lorries were removing and replacing skips as fast as they were filled, but there was still a long queue of cars waiting at the entrance to the tip as we left. Pointing the car towards home, we prepared to run the gauntlet once more through the sweepings and shavings deposited by this mother and father of all storms.

Chapter Twenty

The journey home was no easier or quicker than the outward trip. The hazards were still there but the car was lighter and fresher without the refuse sacks. I'd seen several other walking wounded at the tip, so my black eye hadn't raised any eyebrows, only sympathetic grins.

'Were you frightened last night, Uncle Tom?' asked Paul as we came up to the non-functioning traffic lights, cautiously giving way to a couple of cars before crossing ourselves. Paul waved in acknowledgement to the other drivers, and I mused at how polite and considerate all the drivers were on the road, queuing at the tip, and queuing to leave. Did it require something as momentous as last night's storm for common courtesy to assert itself?

'Were you, Uncle Tom?'

I gave up on my philosophising and realised Paul was waiting for an answer. 'Yes, Paul, I was very frightened last night.' That answer covered a multitude of situations, all of which would be the truth, including the storm.

'And you were all on your own as well. Aunty Jane wasn't there to hold your hand. You should've come over to our house.'

I smiled. 'Yes, I know I could've, but I was alright really, besides which—' Before I could continue, Paul interrupted with all the enthusiasm and worst scenario imaginings of the young.

'You don't think Aunty Jane's plane would've been blown out of the sky, do you? That wind was very strong.'

'No. Aunty Jane's OK. Her plane would've been well out of the way. In fact, by now she should be with Sam, and as soon as the phones are working again, I'm going to give them a ring.'

'If you do, don't forget to tell her she missed a fantastic storm.'

'No, I won't forget,' I said dryly as I turned into the Close and saw Paul safely to his door.

'Looks like we're the first back,' he said scrambling from the car, 'and we had the furthest to go. Bye.'

Garaging the car (the door of which had been a casualty of the storm) I entered the house, checking the telephone on my way through the hall. The familiar drone told me the lines were now in operation. A wave of nausea swept over me, and I clutched at the hallstand, breathing deeply. Another mode of contact for Muffler but at least my mobile was switched off and it was staying that way.

I've no idea how long I stood there until a familiar whine recalled me to my senses. I had to see to the dog. He'd been on his own for far too long. Making my unsteady way to the kitchen (was this going to become my permanent way of walking?), I found him sulking in his basket. His whole attitude one of injured grievance, whether because he'd been abandoned for most of the day, or whether he was just missing Jane, I didn't know. But he did moan, groan and sigh as only he can.

On reflection, I couldn't recall hearing him last night, so the storm obviously hadn't bothered him in the least, knowing Charley he'd probably slept right through it. I know he hadn't moved when I'd been in there. On further reflection he could've howled the house down during the night I wouldn't have heard him – I'd found the oblivion for which I'd craved.

Fully expecting the telephone to ring any moment, I was on edge the whole time I prepared the dog's meal, the smell of which hitting my empty stomach finally made the nausea a reality. Barely making it to the bathroom, I was so violently sick I thought I'd done myself some damage. Retching so hard didn't help my headache one iota, my brain threatening to burst from my skull. Eventually pulling myself together, I splashed cold water over my face and head and returned down the slopes of Everest to let the dog out into the garden.

He went, albeit grudgingly and reluctantly. He'd been anticipating a walk but wild horses, never mind complaining dogs, couldn't have dragged me out again for walkies or anything else. A couple of boiled eggs and some toast washed down with three cups of tea and more painkillers helped settle my stomach. Everything stayed down so I flopped into my chair, a large glass of whisky in my hand, and stared into the fire – or would have done if the dog hadn't plonked himself right in front of it again.

I didn't bother with the television. The noise would have been too intrusive in my thudding head, and I'd had enough storm stories for one day. I also acknowledged to myself that I was perhaps wary of watching the local news in case the fate of Billy and Bobby was the main item. I still wasn't ready to fully face the fact that I was responsible for that fate.

Whatever the reason, I sat in that chair nursing my drink, semi-comatose but with all my nerves on edge waiting for the damn phone to ring. The thought of ringing Jane was simply not on the agenda, I was in no fit state mentally or physically to talk to my wife, and she'd know from the first 'Hello' that something was amiss. No, best leave that until tomorrow when hopefully I'd be more in control. I didn't consider for one moment that Muffler might come round to the house rather than ring – he'd phoned once, he'd phone again. What did he want? He hadn't been to the police, that much was obvious even to an idiot, otherwise they'd have been round here long before now. But what was his game?

'Brr-brr, brr-brr, brr-brr.'

I came to with a jerk spilling what was left of my drink over Charley who looked at me in disgust.

'Brr-brr, brr-brr, brr-brr.'

Moving into the hall like a drunken old man, I picked up the receiver. 'Hello.'

'Hello, Tom?' A woman's voice. My sister. I could've wept with relief. 'Just checking you're alright and the house is still standing. Wasn't it a dreadful night? We lost a chimney pot as well as roof tiles and the front gate. Are you there, Tom, you haven't said a word?'

I actually laughed out loud. 'You must admit, Mary, it's very difficult to get a word in edgeways once you get started.'

'I know. But you sound a trifle weary, are you OK? Have you sustained much damage? Why don't you come over here for a couple of nights, you're very welcome, you know that.'

A trifle weary was probably the understatement of the year, but then my sister had understatements off to a fine art. 'Thanks for the offer but I'm not bad apart from a splitting headache. It's been quite a night and day in one form or another.'

'You can say that again, but I won't keep you now, Tom. I'll ring you tomorrow night. Have you taken anything for your headache?'

'Yes.' I'd lost count of the number or how many more I was likely to take.

'Before I go, Tom, have you heard from Jane yet?'

'No not yet. Tell you what, Mary, I'll give you a call when I get in from work. Sorry about this but my head's really thumping. Bye.' Replacing the receiver, I wondered what Mary's reaction would be if I told her I'd killed two youths. Would she, perhaps for the first time in her life, be rendered speechless? I doubt it. She'd just not believe it. Not her baby brother.

My hand was still on the receiver when it rang again. I must have jumped three feet. The hammer drill in my head began to work even harder with the jerk of my body as I snatched my hand away from the phone.

'Brr-brr, brr-brr.'

Picking up the receiver very gingerly as if it was a scorpion about to deliver a lethal sting, I gave a strangled, 'Hello.'

'Is that ye, Tom, ye do sound strange, man.'

It was Jeff. Relief flooded through me and I sagged against the wall, slowly slipping down until I was sitting on the floor. There was a stinging at the back of my eyes, and I realised it wouldn't take much before I was crying like a baby.

'Tom, what's the matter, have ye had an accident, is it Jane, have ye heard from her? Answer me, Tom, please.'

Taking several deep breaths, I did as he asked and answered him, although I've no idea how I sounded. 'No, Jeff, I haven't heard from Jane, the lines are probably still chaotic. She mightn't have heard about the storm yet anyway, if she is trying to ring, it'll only be to let me know she's arrived safely.' I was waffling or rambling, perhaps they were one and the same thing.

'Something's wrong, Tom. What's happened. It's not the workshop because I've been down there, and we've only lost a few slates.'

The workshop, I hadn't given it a single thought. Not even when I'd said to Mary that I'd ring her after work. That had only been something to say to get her off the phone. I was in a bad way, no doubt about it. Still sitting on the floor, I made a conscious effort to pull myself together and talk to Jeff in as sensible a manner as possible.

'I had a bit of an accident last night. A wayward shed landed in the back garden and a flying plank caught me across the head. It's left me with a black eye and a humdinger of a headache. I can cope with the shiner, the cuts and scratches, but don't seem to be able to get rid of the headache. In fact, if anything, it's getting worse.'

'D'ye think ye should be in hospital? I'll come and take ye to casualty.'

'No, Jeff, don't do that. They must be at capacity level as it is. I'm sure it'll be better after a good night's sleep. It's been a hell of a night and day one way and another.' I gave a small laugh. 'You know I got so involved in helping clear up the Close I never gave a thought to the workshop, or anyone else come to that.'

'Don't ye fret about it none. And don't ye come in tomorrow either, take a few days off. I'll pop around on my way home tomorrow night. But, Tom, are ye sure ye shouldn't go to the hospital, ye could be concussed y'know or even have a fractured skull.'

'I don't think it's that bad. As I say, a good night's sleep may be all that's needed. I'll see how I feel in the morning.'

We said goodbye and his end of the line went dead. I remained on the floor the receiver in my hand. Then the last of my resolve and resistance finally gave up and putting my head in my hands, I sobbed until, like my nausea, there was nothing left. My whole body was shaking and shuddering as I buried my face. I'd likely have remained there indefinitely except I eventually became aware of a new sensation. A warm wet tongue on the back of my exposed neck together with a warm, heavy weight pressing against my shoulder. Charley.

Putting my arm around him, I pressed my face into his fur until I calmed down. He carried on licking the back of my neck and sighing, whether in sympathy or on the vagaries of humans I don't know. But he was my comfort in what I took to be my darkest hour since the killings.

The killings. After my outburst there was a release from all the tensions in my body, and the pressure in my head eased a little. This seemed a good a time as any to face up to what I'd done – to my conscience at least. The telephone receiver was still gripped in my hand. I placed it gently on the floor (I wasn't ready for any more conversations).

Less than 24 hours ago, I had deliberately gone out to kill two people. And had done so. One at least in cold blood. How do you feel, Tom! How did I feel? Hard to say. It was unbelievable to me that I'd been capable of such an act. It could be we're all savages under a thin veneer of civilisation and so-called sophistication.

It was then I acknowledged to myself that I'd finally sunk to the level of those I'd murdered. In the end I was no better than Billy and Bobby. Worse, in fact. The next question was, what was I going to do about it? Stroking the dog's head while I thought, I came to the conclusion I wasn't going to do anything. Not tonight at least. I was in no fit state mentally or physically and felt so traumatised that I'd probably confess to anything at this stage, even to the sinking of the Titanic.

Pushing the dog away, I struggled to my feet and returned to the lounge with the intention of collapsing in my chair but quickly decided I'd be better off in bed. Firstly, I had another long hot soak, wincing as the various bath salts and relaxing unguents attacked the numerous cuts and bruises covering my body. It looked to me as though there were more bruises than clear skin. Headache apart, my knee and neck were giving me the most trouble, irrespective of ministrations earlier on. As I could still bend the knee, I didn't think Bobby's cosh had done any serious damage, but my neck had re-opened hostilities with my skull.

Resorting to the hot milk, whisky and pain killers once again (at this rate I'd probably end up in hospital with an overdose, never mind concussion), I took my weary, battered body up to bed. I was desperate again for a restful dreamless night.

I'd forced myself to listen to the 8pm news on local radio, but there'd been nothing further on the "Bodies in the Dock" as the media had dubbed them. Nor was there mention of any further bodies being found. I suppose three in one place were enough to be going on with. The storm had been responsible for several other fatalities, but they'd been in districts well away from the Quays.

I concluded that two of those bodies in the dock belonged to Billy and Bobby. Common sense told me that Muffler wouldn't have moved them elsewhere for purposes of his own. Perhaps to confront me later! That was too fanciful even for my overwrought mind.

Knowing I was in no fit state to cope with Muffler, I left the phone off the hook, even at the expense of Jane if she should try to get through. Taking my milky cocktail up to bed, I'd hardly drunk it and settled down before I was drifting off, falling into what I fervently hoped would be at least 10 hours of deep, dreamless sleep.

Chapter Twenty-One

It is over. Finished. I am now able to think rationally about the whole horrifying affair. Or to put it another way, I have returned to my senses. Recovered from my temporary insanity.

Three weeks have passed since that fateful night, and once more, I churn the events over in my mind.

The media, of course, made the most of the fact that the storm had been the worst of the twentieth century. One out-of-town hack, in a moment of rhetorical verbiage, christened it the "War of the Elements" a title by which it became known from then on. He made it seem like another film from the *Star Wars* series without the Jedi. Such was the scale of the storm that it far exceeded the nine days wonder of the usual news provoking events.

However, with so many stories of that night in circulation, after a brief flurry in the headlines of the national newspapers, slightly longer in the locals, the "Bodies in the Dock" saga was soon relegated to the inside pages. The story was omitted altogether once it was known the police weren't looking for anyone else in connection with their deaths.

I never heard from Muffler again. My terror, for that's what it was, (I froze each time the telephone rang) proved ground-less for the simple reason that his had been the third body taken from the dock. Three bodies plus Freddie's roof, several cars, numerous rubbish bins, slates and other detritus of the quayside area.

The official line was that Muffler had killed the two youths during a quarrel over drugs, dumping their bodies in the dock and somehow ending up there himself. Perhaps he tripped over his over-long scarf, fell in the dock and was drowned, or maybe the storm played a part in his demise. Who's to know!

I'd forced myself to revisit the scene, ostensibly to see Greg and Jim, but in reality, to see for myself that there were no ghosts hanging round that alleyway. Parking my car at the back, I'd taken a deep breath and walked its length. It was hard to believe I'd stood frozen against that wall, rearranged bins there, picked up a brick perhaps there, and stood waiting for the opportunity to stab two young men to death.

Walking down the length of the entry, I surmised that the force of the storm must have swept both bodies, and everything else in the alleyway, straight into the water, leaving it clear and empty. The rain and wind had done the rest to wash and scour the area clean of any incriminating evidence I may have left. No weapons were ever found, which surprised me, for if they weren't recovered from the bodies, surely they'd have still been in the dock?

That storm which had so battered and bruised my body and picked me up and tossed me around like a rag doll had, unknown to me, also been my salvation. My deus ex machina from both Muffler and the authorities.

Greg's small workforce was working flat out to complete his order as well as trying to clear up the mess left by the "War of the Elements", but Jim immediately stopped what he was doing to make a pot of tea.

'You timed that nicely, Tom,' he said grinning all over his face, 'I was getting desperate trying to think of an excuse to stop for a cuppa.'

'You've only just finished the last one,' said Greg as he shook my hand in greeting.

'At least an hour ago. You ask any of the lads.'

'Don't involve me in your tea wars,' called one of the men as he put on his jacket. 'I'm off to Freddie's for lunch now, Greg. OK?'

'What? Oh, is that the time? We might as well all stop for a bite now.' Greg turned again to me. 'Nice shiner you've got there, Tom. Had an accident with a door?'

'Near enough. A flying garden shed.' I actually believed my own lies these days. 'I see Freddie's still open for business, roof or no roof.'

'I can take a hint,' said Greg as he too put on his jacket. 'A pasty is it, Tom, and two for you, Jim?'

I made to protest but Jim handing me a mug of tea said, 'He's pinching my role and playing the martyr. It's his turn to go.'

Greg laughed as he left. 'Won't be long, I hope. Freddie has a habit of getting his customers to hang onto that tarpaulin covering the roof in case it gets blown away and leaves him exposed again.'

'Freddie's roof was only one of many things that got blown away round here that night,' Commented Jim as the door banged behind Greg and the others. 'You know who it was they fished out of the dock, don't you?'

'Two of them at least and I'd seen them with a third individual over at Freddie's. Was he the other?'

'Yeah. Creepy little bloke he was, always had that great big scarf round his neck.'

'Do you go along with the official explanation of what happened to Billy and Bobby?'

'At first, I couldn't see the point of dumping them there. He always seemed to me to be a very cold fish, not the type to get worked up about the lives of a couple of no-goods like Billy and Bobby. Perhaps a deal went wrong, or they owed him money. He may have lost his cool, bumped them off, panicked and then shoved them in the dock, taking himself and his scarf with them.'

It was slightly disconcerting to find myself having this conversation with Jim. Talking calmly and dispassionately about my victims as if they were so much flotsam and jetsam dredged up out of the dock. In truth, I suppose that's how I'd come to look on them, not as two young men but parasites, takers from society. Always taking never giving.

Jim continued with his story. 'I'd seen them earlier on that day in the cafe. I probably wouldn't have noticed them because they were in a corner, but they were having an argument with another bloke, not the one in the dock, this one was a big, bald fellow. Whatever they were arguing about they didn't get to finish, not inside anyway, for Freddie threw the three of them out. They were still at it when I came back here, and the air was blue with the language the big bloke was using. Now if he'd been found in the water with them, I could've understood it. Perhaps he did the three of them in, whoever he was.'

'But we'll never know what really happened that night will we?' said Greg returning with the pies and catching the end of the conversation. 'It'll remain one of the mysteries of our time, the telling of which will become more vague and distorted as the years go by. The general opinion round here appears to be that they're no great loss to anyone. Except their families,' he added as an afterthought.

So, I'd visited the scene of my crime, and stood at the edge of the dock where, thanks to the indiscriminate force and ferocity of the storm, their bodies had ended up.

My feelings were ambiguous. On the face of it I appeared the same as everyone else. Interested, because I'd worked in the area, had come across them in the cafe and had known them to be a bad lot. But inside I felt different because I'd done the deed. Officially the case may have been closed, but it never would be in my mind.

Physically my cuts and bruises have healed, the way they did after Billy and Bobby attacked me. But mentally the scars will always be there both from what they did and my own actions. I'm not proud of what I did. Could I plead temporary insanity? I certainly didn't behave rationally during that period. I'd thought long and hard before committing murder, so it wasn't a spur of the moment act. It was a straightforward premeditated act of revenge.

Billy and Bobby's way of life had been for kicks and drugs, to take anything and everything their unfortunate victims happened to be carrying. Anything to feed their habit. How many other lives had been marred, as mine had been? How many lives had been ruined and how many others, such as young Mark had ended up dead? Even Sharon, as much as she professed to love Bobby, had been used and abused by him. Their senseless tormenting of Old Dean culminating in the tossing of his coat in the dock had most definitely resulted in his death through exposure. There must be countless others, all unknown, but all suffering through unwelcome contact with the two B's.

Did their upbringing have any bearing on what they'd become, or were they born bad? The old argument of nurture versus nature. I'll never know, nor have I any wish to know now. I only knew what they'd become. If I hadn't ended their reign, who knows how many more innocents would have suffered at their hands, and for how many more years would they have continued! Even the little tart Sharon was as much a victim as the rest of us. Although perhaps she didn't see herself that way and was undoubtedly one of the few, along with his mother, who genuinely mourned Bobby's death. I didn't dare dwell on how "Call me Brenda" would be feeling. If I appear flippant, I could argue that I was only speeding up an inevitable outcome. Or was I playing God!

I firmly believe there are forces for good and evil in this world. At times, the forces for evil gain the upper hand, and in this instance, I'd like to think I've helped redress the balance a little. Sometimes it's necessary to meet force with force.

Machiavelli, that past master of perfidious schemes, wrote that there were two ways of fighting – by law or by force. The first is natural to men and the second to beasts. However, if the first proves inadequate, one must have recourse to the second.

That I had recourse to the second method doesn't make me proud of my actions, and only time will tell whether I'll be able to live with the legacy. But I do know for certain, I'll be able to live with that legacy far better than I lived with the legacy of the attack which started this whole sorry process.

The sun is coming up on the horizon as I look through the window of the plane taking me to New Zealand and my beloved wife and daughter. Lying back in my seat, I close my eyes and know beyond doubt the memory of my actions will always be with me. But the nightmares have gone forever.

Lightning Source UK Ltd.
Milton Keynes UK
UKHW012029080922
408463UK00002B/49